DUST DEVILS

Novels by James Reasoner

TEXAS WIND (available from POINT BLANK)

TIE A BLACK RIBBON by James Reasoner & L.J. Washburn
STARK'S JUSTICE
THE HAWTHORNE LEGACY
THE DIABLO GRANT
WIND RIVER
#2 THUNDER WAGON
#3 WOLF SHADOW
#4 MEDICINE CREEK
#5 DARK TRAIL
#6 JUDGMENT DAY
THE WILDERNESS ROAD
THE HUNTED
UNDER OUTLAW FLAGS

WALKER, TEXAS RANGER:
THE NOVEL
HELL'S HALF ACRE
SIEGE ON THE BELLE

Civil War Battle Series:
Book 1 MANASSAS
Book 2: SHILOH
Book 3: ANTIETAM
Book 4: CHANCELLORSVILLE
Book 5: VICKSBURG
Book 6: GETTYSBURG
Book 7: CHICKAMAUGA
Book 8: SHENANDOAH
Book 9: SAVANNAH
Book 10: APPOMATOX

The Last Good War:
Book 1 BATTLE LINES
Book 2: TRIAL BY FIRE
Book 3: ZERO HOUR

Non-fiction
DRAW: THE GREATEST GUNFIGHTS OF THE AMERICAN WEST

Novels As J. L. Reasoner (with Livia Reasoner)
RIVERS OF GOLD
THE HEALER'S ROAD
HEALER'S CALLING
COSSACK THREE PONIES

DUST DEVILS

James Reasoner

POINTBLANK

Set in Bembo

POINT*BLANK* is an imprint of Wildside Press
www.pointblankpress.com
www.wildsidepress.com

Series Editor JT Lindroos
Editor Allan Guthrie

For more information contact Wildside Press

ISBN: 0-8095-7245-1

One

1.

The cloudless sky was the color of silver. Heat rose in waves from the ground. The road was a ribbon of asphalt laid down across flat, endless fields; two lanes, gravel shoulders.

Water hissed, spraying from irrigation equipment arrayed in the fields bordering the highway, some of it evaporating in the dry air before it ever hit the ground. There were no fences along the road, no cattle here to wander. Only low-lying crops, mostly green, yellowing here and there around the edges, fighting the heat of summer in the Texas Panhandle.

The pickup came out of the haze, passed a sign that read LUBBOCK 76. In the passenger seat, Toby McCoy watched for the turn-off and pretty much ignored the country music coming from the radio and the driver's attempts at conversation. The driver wanted to talk about the chances of his hometown football team once school started again in a few weeks. Toby made polite noises from time to time. After all, the guy was giving him a ride and didn't seem the least bit gay.

"Up there," Toby said. He pointed to a narrow dirt road that led off to the right, forming a perfect ninety degree angle with the highway. "You can let me out there."

The brakes whined as the driver applied them. Toby hadn't seen the turn-off until they were almost on top of it. The pickup rocked to a stop, the front end dipping a little on worn shocks.

Toby opened the passenger door, picked up his duffle bag from the floorboard, swung his legs out and dropped to the shoulder of the road. He looked across the seat at the driver, nodded, and said, "Thanks for the ride."

"You sure you want to get out here, kid? This is the ass-end of no-where."

Toby pointed down the dirt road. "That's where I'm going."

The house was half a mile from the highway, but in this flat country, half a mile was nothing. It was a white-painted frame house that had been there a while, with a detached garage and a barn out back. A few small trees, carefully and faithfully watered against the dry heat, provided a little shade.

The pickup driver lifted a hand in farewell. Toby slammed the door, threw his bag over his shoulder, and walked toward the farmhouse.

He was sweating by the time he got there. A couple of dogs came around the house to bark at him as he approached. One of them was pretty big, with a sleek, tan hide. The other was small, gray, and fuzzy. Toby looked narrow-eyed at the big dog, judging whether or not it was a threat. The dog's tail wagged enough to tell him the animal was friendly despite the loud barking. Toby stuck out a hand, let the dog sniff it, and then scratched behind his ears. The tail wagged harder. The smaller dog just ran around and around, stepping on Toby's feet.

Three cracked concrete steps led up to the front porch. Toby climbed them and went to the door, the boards of the porch creaking a little under his weight. An old metal swing hung on chains from the porch roof. The dogs continued barking at him. He raised his hand to knock on the jamb beside the screen door.

Before he could knock, the inside wooden door opened and a woman looked out at him. She said, "Oh," clearly surprised to find someone standing on the porch. She was blond, pretty, somewhere around forty, wearing jeans and a man's shirt with the sleeves rolled up a couple of turns. She had a dish towel in her hands, and she went back to using it to dry them as she said, "Hello. I heard the dogs pitching a fit. Can I help you?"

She didn't seem frightened by finding a stranger on her front porch. Toby said, "Mrs. Halligan? Mrs. Grace Halligan?"

She finished drying her hands and nodded. "That's right. Something I can do for you?"

"I asked around in Amarillo, and people told me this was your place. Said you might be looking to hire some help, that the last man you had out here up and quit on you."

Toby saw Grace Halligan's eyes move to the edge of the door. Probably looking at the hook. It wouldn't keep out anyone who was determined to get in. She glanced down. Toby looked, too, and saw a tiny sliver of polished wood. The stock of a rifle or shotgun, leaning against the wall beside the door. Grace Halligan was a cautious woman. Living out here on this farm by herself, she would need to be.

She said, "I'm not in the habit of hiring just anybody who walks up—"

"And that's smart. Out here in the middle of nowhere, you don't want to be too trusting. Fact is, if you want me to leave, I'll go right on back down there to the highway and hitch a ride. You can watch me the whole way."

She looked at him for a long moment and then asked, "Who told you I might be hiring?"

"Bob Kingman at Kingman Tractor Supply. Fella I expect sold you that John Deere I saw out by the barn."

She looked past him at the dogs and said, "Max, Clifford, you two hush! That's enough."

The dogs didn't stop barking.

"There's a furnished room back of the garage. I suppose we could give it a try." The words came out slow, reluctant. "I've been short-handed around here since Lupe left. Pay won't be much. I can feed you, though."

"That'll be fine. I'm not looking to get rich."

"What's your name?"

"Toby McCoy."

She reached up and unhooked the screen door. Pushing it with her foot, she opened it enough to stick her hand out.

"Pleased to meet you, Toby."

He shook her hand. "Yes, ma'am. I'm pleased to meet you, too."

"What *are* you looking for?"

"Ma'am?"

"You said you're not looking to get rich. I just wondered what you're looking for instead."

Toby said, "I guess I'll know it when I find it."

2.

Work started early, ended late. And the days were long this time of year. Not like June, when the sun stayed up until nearly nine o'clock at night, but long enough.

Toby didn't mind the work. He liked the tractor, the smell of hot oil and rubber, the roar of the engine, the vibration that went through him when he sat on the black plastic seat that got so hot in the sun it would sear your ass right through your jeans. The rumbling power that he felt as he grasped the steering wheel.

He drove up and down the rows in the fields, pulling the cultivator behind him. The dogs followed along, barking at the tractor but not at him. They had gotten used to having him around in no time at all. Max was the big tan one, Clifford the little gray one. Max liked to dash in and snap at the tractor wheels as they turned. Toby sometimes wondered what Max would do if he turned the steering wheel and drove right at him. Jump out of the way, of course, he decided. The dog was faster than the tractor.

The John Deere was an older model. No enclosed, air-conditioned cab complete with CD player, not even a canopy to give a man some shade. And it broke down fairly often, too. Toby didn't mind. He was good with engines, good with his hands. He was doing productive work. You could tell that just by looking at the fields, which were shaping up just fine under his care. He didn't even mind when he had to take a hoe and work some of the crops by hand. A callus or two formed on his palms. He looked on them as badges of honor.

There was more to taking care of the farm than just tending the fields. Mrs. Halligan had some livestock: a few pigs in a pen, a couple of milk cows, a handful of chickens. They had fresh milk and eggs all the time, something Toby had never known before. He slopped the hogs, fed the cows and the chickens.

He knew Mrs. Halligan was keeping an eye on him. When he crawled out from under the tractor, smeared with grease from working on the engine, she was on the back porch. When he came in from the fields and went to his room behind the garage, her eyes followed him from the kitchen window. When he carried buckets of scraps out to the hogs, she was in her vegetable garden, watching him.

At first she hadn't trusted him. He was sure of that and not surprised by it. But as the days passed, she relaxed more and more. Sometimes when he caught her looking at him, she smiled, and he grinned back at her. She would shake her head then, as if amazed that he was such a hard worker.

He drove the tractor in from the fields one afternoon and saw her through the kitchen window, standing over the sink. Leaving the engine running, he jumped to the ground, went to the barn, opened the doors. There was a cloud coming up, maybe. Panhandle storms were rare this time of year, but when they came, they brought thunder and lightning, the occasional tornado, and torrents of rain. He wanted to put the tractor inside for the night. He climbed back on, drove into the barn.

By the time he shut the engine off, Grace Halligan was standing just outside the open double doors.

"Toby?"

"Yes, ma'am?" He hopped down and came toward her. "You need something, Mrs. Halligan?"

"Why don't you call me Grace? You've been eating your meals in your room. Why don't you have supper in the house with me tonight? I'm cooking a pot of chili."

The words came out just slightly rushed, as if she wanted to get it all said before something happened to stop her, or before she thought better of it.

"That sounds really good. Are you sure it'd be all right?"

"You've been here for two weeks, working as hard as any hand I've ever had, and you've been a perfect gentleman. I'd be glad to have you to supper."

"Thank you. It'd be my pleasure to come."

"About seven?"

"Yes, ma'am. I mean Grace."

She turned and walked toward the house with the dogs following her. Toby watched her go, saw the glance she threw over her shoulder at him. He nodded, lifted a hand, waved a little, called out, "Seven."

She waved back at him. He looked at the sky, mostly clear but with a dark line of cloud on the northern horizon, and went to close the barn doors. He whistled a little to himself as he swung them shut.

3.

Wind whipped up a dust devil in front of the barn as Toby walked from his room behind the garage over to the back door of the house. The clouds had edged down, spreading from the north into the west, obscuring the lowering sun. It made for an early dusk.

The shower in the furnished room was cramped and the pipes rattled when the water was turned on. The water pressure was weak, the water itself tepid at best and a little rusty, with a faint odor of sulfur clinging to it, but it served to wash off the dust and grit. Toby's hair was still damp. He wore a clean pair of jeans and a short-sleeved khaki work shirt. He went up to the back door and knocked.

A moment later, Grace opened the wooden door and pushed back the screen. "You should've just come on in," she said. She wore jeans, as usual, but instead of a man's shirt she had on an actual blouse. It was the color of peaches. The spicy fragrance of the chili filled the kitchen, along with cold air pumped out by the big swamp cooler set in a side window.

"I didn't want to make myself too much at home," Toby said as he closed the doors behind him.

"Well, that's considerate of you. I hope you don't mind eating in the kitchen. Opening up the dining room seemed like too much trouble."

"Eating in the kitchen is fine," Toby told her. "Growing up, I never ate anywhere else."

The chili simmered in a big pot on the stove. He knew Grace was a good cook. She had brought several casseroles out to his room during the time he had been here. The old, formica-topped table was set with flower-patterned plates, heavy silverware, and tall, sweat-beaded glasses of iced tea. A loaf of homemade bread wrapped in a dish towel sat beside the plates. Grace took a knife from a drawer, uncovered the bread, and was about to slice it when she stopped and looked up at Toby.

"There are crackers if you'd rather have them. I know some people like crackers with their chili, or Fritos, but I've always eaten bread with mine."

The bread smelled good. Toby said, "No, this is fine."

She cut several slices of bread and put two on each plate. Then she ladled chili from the pot into bowls that matched the plates and put them next to the bread.

"I'm afraid there's nothing fancy about this meal," she said.

"It smells great. Thank you for inviting me."

"Well ... sit down and dig in, I guess."

The chili was just right, pretty spicy but not hot enough to blister your tongue. The bread was sweet and warm. As they ate, the wind blew harder outside, hard enough so that Toby heard it over the rumble of the swamp cooler. He was waiting for the rain, but so far it hadn't started to fall.

"Where are you from?" Grace asked, then added, "If I'm not prying too much."

"Not at all. I'm from Oklahoma City."

"You have family there? Do your parents live there?"

Toby shook his head. "My parents passed away a while back. I don't have any other relatives, so I've been on my own since then."

She put her spoon down and looked across the table at him. "I'm sorry."

"That's all right. I'm doing okay."

"You know, when I first saw you, I thought to myself that you ought to be in college somewhere. I guess ... I guess that's why you're not."

"College costs a lot of money. I managed to finish high school, but anything else ... That'll just have to wait."

"You've been working ever since?"

"Yes, ma'am. I mean Grace. Two years of doing odd jobs, working in fast food joints, stuff like that. I never liked it much. And since there was nothing back home to keep me tied down, I decided to come over here to the Panhandle and see some place new."

"If you wanted to see something, the Panhandle's not much. Just miles and miles of flat nothing."

"It's not that bad. There are places like this. You've got grass and trees."

"Takes a deep well and a lot of watering to keep them going, too."

"Well, I like it so far," Toby said. "I think it's mighty pretty around here."

He gave her an honest, open smile as he spoke, and after a second she looked down into her bowl. He saw her face redden a little. Not much, just enough to tell him that she was blushing. She concentrated on eating for a few minutes, letting whatever had sprung up in the air between them dissipate.

When she spoke again, she asked, "Do you think you'll stay long?"

"I guess that depends on how long it takes me to wear out my welcome."

4.

The storm still hadn't blown in by the time they finished eating. They sat on the sofa in the living room and watched TV for a while, but Grace didn't have cable or a satellite dish and only two stations came in, one from Lubbock and one from Amarillo, both of them pretty fuzzy.

"You must be bored to death out here, a young man like you," Grace said. "There's nothing to do, and you can't even watch TV much."

"That's the good thing about working all day long. Time you're finished, you're tired, and it doesn't take much to entertain you. I've got a little radio. Mostly I just sleep."

"Well, any time you want to watch TV, you're welcome to. Sometimes there's a baseball game on, and I guess football will be starting up again pretty soon."

"Thanks. I've never been much of a sports fan, though."

He got up a little while after that and said that he ought to be getting back to his room. Grace walked to the back door with him. Lightning flickered off in the distance, so far away the thunder was more of a whisper than a rumble.

"Good night," she said as he started toward the garage.

He looked back at her and said, "Good night … Grace."

5.

It didn't rain at all that night, even though Toby heard the thunder off and on until not long before dawn. The storms all went around the farm. When he started out to do the morning chores, the sky was clear again, the clouds all having moved on to the south.

The heat started in early, grew through the morning, blazed on into afternoon. His shirt was sodden with sweat as he bounced along on the tractor, so he took it off and draped it over the seat back behind him. The sun was molten on his skin, but he preferred that to the sticky-wet shirt.

When he drove to the barn and cut off the engine, the back door of the house opened and Grace came out carrying a pitcher of iced tea and a glass. She walked over as he climbed down from the tractor. Every muscle in his body felt loose. She filled the glass from the pitcher and handed it to him. He raised it to his lips, drank deeply.

"Man, that's good," he said when he lowered the glass. "It must be a hundred and five today."

"You're going to blister without a shirt."

"Nah, I never blister."

"Well, you'd better cool off before you go back out there."

He drank the rest of the tea, the ice cubes clinking against the glass.

"I'll rinse off with the hose," he said as he handed the glass to her.

A garden hose was coiled next to the concrete foundation of the house. Grace used it every day to water her vegetable garden. Toby picked up the hose, turned on the faucet it was attached to, and put his thumb over the end of the hose, making the water spray out. He bent over and played the water over his head and torso, soaking himself.

"Boy, that feels good!" He shook his head, water droplets flying off his face and hair.

Grace laughed. "You certainly look like you're enjoying it."

He looked over at her. A mischievous grin appeared on his face.

Grace started to back away. "Don't you dare!" she said, but she was smiling, too. She let out a cry as Toby turned the spray on her. Laughing, she ran for the back steps as he continued squirting her with the hose. When she got there she set the pitcher and glass down and then turned back to dart toward the faucet, intending to turn it off.

Toby whooped and hit her harder with the spray, soaking her shirt and jeans. She thrust a hand out as if to fend off the water, but it didn't do any good. Sputtering from a mouthful of water she had gotten accidentally, she veered away from the faucet and lunged toward Toby instead.

"If that's the way you want to play!" she said as she grabbed at the hose. She got hold of it and tried to turn the spray toward him, but he was too strong. Both of them laughed as they struggled over it.

Then Grace abruptly quit fighting. She stood there, only inches from his bare, wet chest. Her shirt was plastered to her, and her bra was plainly visible through the soaked fabric. She pushed a strand of wet hair out of her face and lifted her head to look at him. Neither of them laughed now, and their smiles were gone.

Toby dropped the hose. The water puddled unnoticed around their feet. He put a hand under her chin and leaned over to kiss her. Their bodies didn't touch, only their lips and his hand on her chin. The kiss was tentative at first, before growing more urgent, but it lasted only a moment. Grace pulled away. Toby didn't try to stop her.

She turned and ran for the back door, not even stopping to pick up the pitcher of iced tea and the glass as she hurried inside.

"Grace!"

The door slammed behind her.

Toby looked down at his hand. He had lifted it, held it out toward her as if to stop her, without even being aware of it. He lowered it now, sighed, bent to turn off the water at the faucet.

6.

It was evening before he saw her again. Wearing clean clothes, he left the garage room and walked around the house to the front. Max and Clifford lay on the porch. They lifted their heads as he came up the steps.

"Well, at least neither of you growled at me," he said to them.

He went to the door and knocked on it. There was no response from inside.

"Grace? Grace, I'm sorry. I never meant to do anything to offend you. Grace?"

Still no answer.

"If you want, I'll just get my stuff and go."

The wooden door opened, but the screen stayed shut. The inside of the house was dim, with no lights burning in the thickening dusk.

"No," she said softly. "Don't go."

Toby moved toward the door. "Grace, I'm sorry—"

"It wasn't your fault. I'm twice your age. I should have known better."

"You don't seem twice my age. You seem, I don't know, the same as me. That's why I like talking to you so much."

She gave a hollow laugh. "You weren't talking this afternoon."

"I know." He sounded miserable. "I don't know why I … It's just that you're so pretty and so nice." Now he took a step back away from the door. "I really think I ought to just leave."

She opened the screen door and took half a step onto the porch. In the last fading light of day he saw that she wore a robe, belted tight around her waist. She lifted a hand toward him.

"No, Toby, you don't have to go. I … I want you to stay."

He looked at her for a long moment, searching her face, her eyes, making certain that he saw what he thought he saw.

"You're sure?"

"I'm sure."

And just like that, nothing could ever be the same between them again. She reached out and put her hand on his arm, rested it there for a second, and then slid it down so that she took his hand. Her fingers laced together with his. The space between them went away. Toby kissed her again. Her other hand reached up and found the back of his neck, held it. They moved into the darkened house, the screen door banging quietly behind them.

7.

Moonlight slanted through the gap between the curtains and silvered the bed and the two figures moving on it.

Toby had been able to tell right from the start that Grace had a good body under those jeans and men's shirts she wore most of the time. But even so he had been a little surprised at the tautness of her flesh when he touched it. Her breasts were still firm, her thighs sleek and muscular, and when he slid into her he knew she hadn't been fucked for quite a while. She was tight and wet and eager, and she cried out in orgasm not once but twice before he came in her.

Then she sighed a long, shuddery sigh and clutched him tightly to her. He kissed her shoulder, rolled onto his back. She snuggled into his side and pulled his arm over her as if he were the one older than her, as if he would hold her and protect her from all the ills of the world. He stared up at the ceiling, listening to her breathe for a long time before he knew she was asleep.

Two

1.

Grace hadn't turned the light on the night before when they went to her bedroom, so Toby didn't get a good look at his surroundings until the next morning when the sun came up.

Grace was normally an early riser, up before dawn, but this morning she was still sound asleep as the reddish-gold glow filled the room. Toby lay beside her and watched her sleep for a few minutes, then turned his head and looked around.

The wallpaper was beige with green vines twisting up through it and some sort of little flowers. A chest of drawers sat against the wall beside the window. On the other side of the room, on the wall next to the door, was a dresser with a wood-framed mirror attached to the top of it. A photograph was stuck behind one corner of the mirror frame. The chest, the dresser, and the bed all matched, made out of the same sort of blond, heavily varnished wood. Toby didn't know what kind of wood it was. He had never been any good at remembering things like that.

There was a rocking chair in one corner with cushions tied onto the seat and back, the strings that fastened them on dangling. A straight-backed chair was pushed up into the kneehole of the dresser.

The floors were hardwood, but there were thick rugs on both sides of the bed and in front of the closet door. A couple of pictures on the walls, anonymous prints of English countryside scenes. A small stack of paperback books on top of the chest. Toby couldn't make out the titles from the bed, but they were thick and had the look of glossy bestsellers. A few knick-knacks on the dresser, a snow globe, a music box, things like that. It was the room of someone who didn't have a completely empty life, but not a particularly full one, either.

Carefully so as not to disturb her sleep, he slipped out of bed and looked around for his underwear. Spotting them on the floor, he bent, picked them up, stepped into them. Barefooted, silent, he walked around the room to take a closer look at the furnishings. When he came to the dresser, he picked up the snow globe, shook it, set it down. It didn't have enough snow in it. When he'd been a kid, snow globes had had more snow in them.

The photograph stuck in a corner of the mirror frame caught his attention. He leaned closer to it to study it. Two women were in the photograph, and one of them was Grace. The other woman looked older, with gray streaks in her dark hair and features that were drawn and faded. She gave the camera a tired smile. There was no family resemblance between her and Grace, but oddly enough, the older woman seemed familiar somehow. He considered taking the photograph off the mirror and turning it over to see if any names were written on the back, but he thought he might not be able to get it back like he had found it.

He reached down and eased open one of the dresser drawers. Underwear was piled inside it in disarray, bras and panties jumbled together. Most of the panties were made of cotton, but he pawed through them until he found a pair made of silk. He slid his fingertips over the smooth fabric and enjoyed the sensation. Then he replaced them in the drawer and pushed them down so that Grace would be less likely to notice that he had been in there.

He touched something hard beneath the underwear.

Frowning a little, Toby gave in to his curiosity and pushed panties aside until he uncovered a pistol. It was a stubby, ugly-looking automatic, the same size as a Saturday night special but higher quality than that, a well-made little piece of wickedness. Not at all the sort of thing he would have expected to find hidden in the underwear drawer of a farm woman in the middle of the Texas Panhandle.

Grace stirred in the bed.

Toby pulled the panties back over the gun and soundlessly shut the drawer. He turned toward the bed and saw that her eyes were still closed. She was lying on her stomach. The sheet was pushed back enough so that he could see the side of one breast. He went over to the bed and sat down beside her.

She rolled over, opened her eyes, and looked up at him. He said, "Good morning."

"Good morning yourself."

"How are you?"

"Oh, I'm fine." She stretched, lifting her breasts. "I'm just fine."

His face wore a solemn expression as he said, "Listen, Grace, last night was wonderful, but if you want me to leave, I'll understand."

"Did I say I wanted you to leave?"

"No, but—"

"Then stop talking about it." She reached up, looped an arm around his neck, and pulled him toward her. "Sorry if I've got morning breath, honey, but you come here."

She kissed him, and his hand went to one of her breasts, cupping and squeezing it. She pushed his underwear down to get at his penis, wrapped her fingers around it, and sighed against his mouth as she felt how hard and ready he was.

He threw the sheet back and moved quickly between her legs.

2.

"You go ahead and eat," she said as she put the plateful of scrambled eggs, toast, and bacon in front of him. There was so much food he couldn't see the little flowers on the plate.

"What about you?" he asked.

She sat down on the other side of the table with a cup of coffee. Tendrils of steam rose from the cup.

"I'm fine. I'm not really hungry yet. I'll eat something later." She sipped the coffee. "I never have been much of one for eating breakfast. But you wouldn't know that, would you, Toby?"

"No, ma'am," he said around a mouthful of toast and bacon.

Grace laughed. "What have I told you about ... Never mind. You can call me ma'am any time you want."

Toby ate a few more bites and then set his fork down beside the plate. He sipped from his own cup of coffee and said, "You know, I never expected this."

"You mean bacon and eggs?"

"I mean what happened between us. It's like something out of a bad country song."

"Things happen. Just because somebody sings about them doesn't mean they don't."

"Yeah, but I can still leave if you want."

She reached across the table to place her hand on his. "You really have to stop saying that," she told him. "I want you to stay. Don't you ever forget that. I want you to stay."

3.

He had fed the dogs, milked the cows, and thrown a bucketful of scratch to the chickens by the time Grace came out the back door carrying the egg basket. She went into the barn. A row of coops was built along one wall. Toby knew it would take her a while to collect the eggs. He knew how long it took her to perform all the chores around the place.

He waited until she was out of sight and then went to the back door of the house. The screen door hinges squealed a little as he opened them. Should have oiled them, he told himself, but he didn't think the noise was loud enough for her to have heard it in the barn.

He went through the kitchen, down the hall past the unused dining room, and into the living room. When they had watched TV in there a couple of nights earlier, he had seen the desk in the corner with the computer sitting on it. A light glowed on the computer, showing that its power was on. He sat down in the swivel chair in front of the desk, turned on the monitor, rolled the mouse to wake up the computer. The screen came to life.

It took him only a few minutes to go through Grace's files. They didn't contain anything out of the ordinary. An income tax program told him that the farm had made a profit of $8,764 the year before. The only thing in her e-mail folder was some undeleted spam.

He turned the monitor off and started going through the desk drawers. Envelopes, rubber bands, paperclips, a file of paid bills. No letters, nothing personal. He started to remove the center drawer, but as he did, something about it felt odd to him. He bent to look underneath it.

A revolver was taped to the bottom of the drawer, held in place by two strips of duct tape that formed an X over it.

Toby shook his head as he pushed the drawer back where it was supposed to be. That was the second gun he had found in an unusual place. He glanced at the front door, saw the shotgun leaning against the wall. He had never expected to find so many weapons in the house. What was Grace afraid of?

One drawer remained that he hadn't searched. He pulled it open. More meaningless papers. He sorted through them, lifting out handfuls, and finally at the bottom he found what he was looking for. He took it out and piled everything else back into the drawer.

It was a small scrapbook, the kind that could be bought in any drugstore. He sat back in the chair, put the scrapbook in his lap, and opened it.

The first thing he saw was a lock of hair in a sealed plastic bag that had been fastened to one of the pages with strips of tape that had yellowed with age. The hair was long and fine, with just a little curl to it, brown shading to blond in color. He wasn't surprised at the color. He knew that many babies had fairer hair when they were born than they did later in life.

A piece of paper had been taped to the opposite page. It had a pair of tiny inked footprints on it. He looked at them for a long moment. Somebody had touched one of the prints when it was fresh, so that the ink was smeared in one spot near the heel. Toby wondered who had done that.

He took a deep breath and turned the page. A several-months-old baby looked up at him from a 5X7 photograph. The baby's hair matched that of the lock in the plastic bag. He had a serious look on his pudgy face, and his eyes were a little red as if he had been crying. The photographer must have worked and waited for quite a while, trying with toys and goofy faces to get the kid to smile, before finally giving up and snapping the photo while the baby at least wasn't yowling.

Toby didn't look at anything else in the scrapbook, because he had lost track of time and because he was so intent on the photograph that he didn't hear Grace's footsteps, didn't even know she had come into the room until she said from behind him, "Find what you're looking for?"

4.

Toby didn't jump, didn't show any reaction. All that was clamped down tight. He turned, the chair seat swiveling, the scrapbook still in his hands.

"Hello, Grace."

She stood just inside the door from the hall into the living room. Her face was cold and hard, her mouth tight, her eyes angry but also hurt. At least she hadn't picked up the shotgun before confronting him. Her hands were empty. She said, "You'd better tell me why you're going through my things. Are you looking for something to steal?"

"I'm not a thief," he said.

"Then what are you doing?"

"Exploring history." He could see that the answer took her by surprise. He lifted the scrapbook and went on, "Ancient history. Twenty years ago, to be precise."

She came a step closer to him. "What the hell are you talking about?"

"This little boy here." He turned the scrapbook so that she could see the photograph. "Did you even give him a name? Or were you in such a hurry to get rid of him that you didn't bother?"

Her eyes widened in surprise. "Toby—"

He couldn't keep the anger out of his voice now, no matter how hard he tried. "Did you just put Baby Boy Winston on the birth certificate? Did you think that because you changed your name and moved to Texas I couldn't find you?"

Now instead of coming forward she backed away a step. She lifted a hand, held it out toward him. "Toby, you don't understand—"

He came to his feet and flung the scrapbook across the room. She flinched as it slammed into the wall.

"The hell I don't understand … Mom! You thought I'd never find you, didn't you?"

"Toby, no. You don't know—"

He interrupted her again, in no mood now to listen to explanations. "This is the age of the Internet. There are all sorts of ways to trace birth parents these days."

He came across the room toward her, thinking she might turn and run, but she didn't move as he grabbed her arms and pulled her toward him.

"I guess this makes me a real mother fucker, doesn't it?"

"You bastard!"

"You'd know, wouldn't you?"

He had been planning for weeks what he would say when he finally confronted her, and she had cooperated beautifully, even giving him a good line he could ad-lib off of. He saw the shock and pain in her eyes and drank it in, relishing it, taking it as his due for all the years of loneliness, all the years of knowing that he had been abandoned.

It felt so good that he wasn't watching her closely enough, so he didn't have time to get out of the way as her knee came up into his groin. It smashed into his balls and sent red agony flooding through him. He cried out and bent over, letting go of her arms.

She put her hands on his shoulders and shoved hard, sending him reeling back onto the sofa. He clutched at himself and tried not to cry. He hated crying.

She didn't look surprised and shocked anymore. She just looked furious as she said, "You idiot! You've got it all wrong! I'm not your mother!"

Toby hurt too much to argue with her, and anyway, there wasn't time, because that was when the front door crashed open and a man came through it with a gun in his hand.

5.

The gun was a big revolver, and it gleamed in the man's hand as he swung it toward Grace and fired. The roar was so loud it slammed against Toby's ears like fists. He cried out, expecting to see blood and brains explode from Grace's head.

But Grace wasn't where she had been. She had thrown herself forward in a rolling dive toward the desk. The man jerked the gun toward her and fired again, but he rushed the shot and the bullet smashed the computer monitor instead.

Grace lay on her back in front of the desk. She reached up into the kneehole and grabbed the gun fastened to the underside of the middle drawer. It came loose with a ripping of tape.

As soon as she had the gun in her hand, Grace moved again, rolling to the side. The big revolver blasted for a third time, just as the smaller gun cracked. The man who had kicked in the front door grunted and took a step backward. He managed to get off a fourth shot, but it plowed harmlessly into the wall. Grace shot him twice more, once in the chest and once in the head. Blood welled from the black hole in his forehead as he went over backward to crash down in a heap in the shattered doorway, half in the house and half on the porch.

Toby had forgotten all about how bad his balls hurt.

Grace scrambled to her feet. "Help me!" she said to Toby. "We have to get him inside."

He lay there unmoving on the sofa, gaping at her. His ears rang from the deafening gunshots, and he wasn't completely sure he hadn't been hit by any of the bullets flying around the room. He didn't think he had, but he wanted to check himself over before he admitted that he was okay.

"Damn it, come on," Grace said as she went over to the body. "We don't have much time. He wouldn't come here alone."

Before Toby could move, another man stepped into the room from the hall, behind Grace. He had a pump shotgun in his hands, and he worked the mechanism and lined the barrel on her back.

"Don't move, Dana," he said. "Drop the gun."

She stiffened but didn't look around at him. "Hans?"

"That's right. So you know I'll kill you if I have to."

Grace bent over slowly and placed her gun on the floor. As she straightened, Hans moved farther into the room. He was tall and lean and had graying blond hair. Eyes like flint flicked toward Toby.

"Who's the boy?"

"He says he's my son," Grace said.

"Really?" Hans arched a thin eyebrow. "I never knew you had a child."

"Life's full of surprises."

Toby swallowed. There was an air of intense unreality about the whole thing. Grace and the man called Hans were standing there talking casually, even though there was a dead man lying in the doorway and Hans had a shotgun pointed at Grace's back. Somehow the oddity of it made it even more frightening.

"I'm sorry about Roy," Hans said. "He was a good man."

Grace made a contemptuous noise. "If he was any good, he wouldn't have come in shooting. He never did have any patience."

"I told him we needed you alive, but his anger at what you did to us got the better of him, I suppose. In that way, I'm glad he missed." Hans paused. "Now, to business."

"I don't have any business with you," Grace said.

"I beg to differ. There's a little matter of four hundred thousand dollars."

Toby heard that clearly enough, despite the ringing in his ears. Hans hadn't threatened him with the shotgun, and the other man was dead. Toby sat up.

"Grace, what's he—"

Hans turned smoothly toward him. "Don't move! I need her alive, not you."

"Leave him alone," Grace said. "He doesn't have anything to do with this. There's no need to hurt him."

"I don't wish to hurt anyone. You know that. I just want the money."

"I don't have it."

"Don't lie to me, Dana. I always knew when you were lying."

Grace laughed. "Honey, you never had a clue."

Hans kept the shotgun pointed at Toby, who wished he would point it somewhere else. But he looked back toward Grace, and as he did he could see out the picture window as well. Curtains covered the window, but there was a gap between them that showed the dirt road leading to the farm house from the highway. Toby saw the angry expression on Hans's face replaced by a worried one.

"Someone is coming!" Hans edged toward the front window. "My God. It's a fucking cop."

He turned and jabbed the barrel of the shotgun toward Grace. His eyes were a little wild now.

"Why are the police coming here?"

"I don't know," Grace said with a shake of her head. "I swear it. You know I wouldn't call the cops out here, Hans."

Hans jerked the shotgun toward Toby. "You! Boy! Pull that body in here."

Toby swallowed and said, "Grace …?"

"You'd better do what he says," she told him.

Toby stood up from the sofa, feeling a strange weakness in his knees and his guts as he did so. He fought off the fear and went over to the corpse. Roy, that was what Hans had called him. Roy with the open staring eyes and the worm of blood crawling across his forehead and the bigger bloodstain on his chest.

Hans backed off a little so that he could cover both Grace and Toby with the shotgun. Toby bent over and took hold of Roy's ankles. They felt the same dead as they would have alive. He grunted with effort as he dragged the heavy corpse completely inside the living room. The front door would close now, even though the shattered lock probably wouldn't catch.

Hans moved past the body to the door and pushed it closed. He checked the view from the picture window again. Toby looked, too, and saw the highway patrol car that was plainly visible as it approached on the dirt road.

"Get rid of him," Hans said to Grace. "I'll be right here with the boy, and I'll kill him if you don't do as you're told."

"Take it easy," she said. "Whatever's going on here, it doesn't have anything to do with you."

She stepped onto the porch and pulled the door closed behind her. Toby and Hans watched through the gap in the curtains as the highway patrol car stopped in front of the house. Only one officer was in it. He opened the door and got out. He wore black uniform trousers, a gray uniform shirt, a black tie. He put a cream-colored Stetson on his head as he walked toward the house.

Inside the living room the air was hot and still, weighted with tension. It stank of burned powder and blood. The front door was open just enough so that Toby could hear the officer's voice as he greeted Grace.

"Mornin', ma'am. Would you be Mrs. Halligan?"

"That's right," she said. "What can I do for you?"

The officer came closer. "I was sent out here to give you some news, ma'am. Now, I don't want you to worry, but—" He stopped short, looked at the floor of the porch, and frowned. "What's that?"

Toby craned his neck to look, saw that the blood from Roy's wounds had puddled and begun to run under the door. Not much of it could have seeped onto the porch by now. Maybe the officer was looking at something else.

"That looks like blood!"

Or not.

The officer reached for the pistol holstered on his hip and said, "Get down, ma'am!"

Before the gun was halfway out of the holster, the front window exploded outward as Hans fired the shotgun through it. Shards of glass sprayed everywhere. The load of buckshot caught the officer in the chest and threw him against his car. Momentum bent him backward over the hood. The front of his shirt was already black with blood. His hat flew off his head, landed upside-down on the hood, and spun around a little. The officer hung there on the car for a second, then slid off and tumbled face-down to the ground.

Hans pumped the shotgun and went right up to the shattered picture window, pushing aside the buckshot-torn tatters of the curtains so that he could lean forward and cover the fallen officer. The barrel of the shotgun stuck out through the opening.

Grace was still on the porch. She moved almost too fast for Toby's eyes to follow as she grabbed the barrel of the shotgun with her left hand and forced it down, at the same time catching hold of Hans's shirt with her right hand and jerking him forward through the window. He screamed as the jagged glass in the frame sliced into him. Grace pulled him all the way through the window and kicked him in the head. He sprawled on the porch.

He still had hold of the shotgun and tried to lift it. Grace grabbed the metal swing and slammed it into his face, cutting his cheek to the bone. She kicked him again, this time catching him on the wrist so that the shotgun was knocked out of his hand.

She hadn't knocked all the fight out of him, despite the damage she had inflicted. He brought a leg around, sweeping her feet out from under her. She fell and landed hard on her right hip. He lunged at her, using his weight to knock her onto her back. His hands clawed at her throat as he tried to choke her. Grace struggled to pull his fingers loose but couldn't stop him from getting a good grip. He bounced her head off the porch as he strangled her.

Toby watched wide-eyed from the window as he tried to figure out what to do. He could let Hans kill Grace, but once she was dead, Hans would probably try to kill him next. He turned around to look for the big revolver that Roy had dropped.

A gurgling sound made him look back at the porch. Grace had gotten her hand on one of the large pieces of glass that had come from the broken window and driven it into Hans's throat. Blood splashed over her face as it spurted from the wound in his neck. He let go of her and pawed feebly at the shard of glass, dislodged it. Even more blood came out. He fell to the side and kicked and gurgled some more as he died.

Grace pushed herself out from under his legs and backed rapidly away from him, scooting over the porch on her butt. When she reached the shotgun, she grabbed it and stood up. The barrel swung toward Toby.

He figured he was a dead man. Grace's lips were pulled back from her teeth in a grimace, her face was covered with blood, there was even blood in her tangled blond hair. He just knew she was going to shoot him.

Instead, she said, "Get out here!"

Toby's pulse raced wildly, but the fact that he was still alive said something to him. Maybe she wouldn't kill him after all. He stepped over Roy's body, opened the door, and went out onto the porch.

"I haven't forgotten about what you did, but right now I want you to check that cop, see if he's still alive."

"I … I don't know how."

"See if there's a pulse in his neck, for God's sake! You're no good to me if you get sick or freeze up, damn it."

Toby made calm-down motions with his hands. "Okay. Okay."

He went down the steps and walked over to the highway patrol officer. The ground under the man was dark with blood. Toby felt for a pulse, didn't find one. He checked again just to make sure, then looked up at Grace and shook his head.

"He's dead, all right."

"You're sure?"

"Yeah. What about Hans?"

"Don't worry about him. He won't ever bother anybody again."

"Grace ... Mom ..." He was seized with an almost uncontrollable urge to laugh as he thought about using that name for the blood-covered, shotgun-wielding, crazy woman on the porch. "What's all this—"

"Don't call me that!" she said. "I told you I'm not your mother."

He frowned. "But ... you're Grace Halligan. You said so yourself."

"I lied. Get the cop's pistol and any other weapons you can find in his car."

Toby hesitated before doing as she told him, looked over at Hans's body. "He called you Dana. I heard him."

"Forget about that for now. Just get the damned guns." She took a deep breath and pushed the blood-smeared hair out of her face. "We're liable to need all the firepower we can get."

Three

1.

Grace wiped blood off her face with a rag as she led Toby into the bedroom. She told him, "Grab some of my clothes and stuff them into the suitcase you'll find under the bed. I don't care what it is, just something to wear. I've got to take a shower and wash off this blood."

"You're worried about HIV?"

She laughed. "No. Hans never used drugs, and he didn't care about sex. Said it interfered with his concentration and he couldn't afford that. All he was really interested in was money. The blood's just sticky. I want it off me."

Toby didn't blame her for feeling that way. He bent over, reached under the bed, and felt around for the suitcase she had mentioned. He jerked his hand back as if he had touched a snake.

"What's wrong?" Grace asked.

Toby reached under the bed again and pulled out a high-powered rifle. He couldn't help but think about how they had had sex on that bed the night before, and that very morning, too.

"This isn't a farm house, it's a goddamn arsenal."

Grace had tugged her blood-soaked shirt out of her jeans and peeled it off. She threw it in a corner.

"Tools of the trade," she said.

Toby found a battered suitcase under the bed. He pulled it out, set it on the bed, opened it. No guns or hand grenades. He started packing clothes from the dresser into it, shoving them in haphazardly.

"What are you, some sort of hitwoman? My mom, the killer?"

Grace had the rest of her clothes off by now. Hans's blood had soaked through in places, leaving her with faint red splotches on her breasts and stomach.

"I told you to stop calling me that." She pointed to the other woman in the photograph tucked in a corner of the mirror frame. "That's your mother."

Toby stopped stuffing underwear and shirts into the suitcase and looked at the picture. "But when I first came here, you said you were Grace Halligan."

"I know what I said. But that's Grace Halligan. My name is Dana Carson."

It was finally starting to soak in on him. "So you're really not my mother."

"No." She stood there naked and bloody and strangely calm now. "But you're still a dumb motherfucker anyway."

2.

She didn't take long in the shower. When she came out she was toweling her hair dry. Toby sat on the bed next to the suitcase and watched her.

"I should have known better than to get mixed up with you," she said as she went to the closet and picked out a shirt and a pair of jeans. "I did know better. But it had been so long …"

"You owe me an explanation."

"Maybe later." She took underwear out of the drawer, lifted out the little automatic pistol as well and set it on top of the dresser. "Right now we don't have much time."

He took a deep breath. "I think we should call the police."

The glance she gave him told him just how unlikely that was to happen. "They'll be here soon enough when that state trooper doesn't call in. And they won't be the only ones."

"What do you mean?"

"You don't think Hans and Roy were the only guys looking for me, do you?"

Toby hadn't thought about that. He stood up and said, "I'll get my stuff ready to go."

"That would be a good idea."

"I don't have much."

"I know."

He went out the back, not wanting to go through the front where the bodies of Hans and Roy and the state trooper lay in the living room where he and Grace—no, Dana—had put them. It was going to take him a while to get used to thinking of her that way. For more than two weeks, he had believed she was Grace Halligan, had believed that she used to be Donna Winston of Oklahoma, who had given birth to a baby boy and then abandoned him. But clearly, nothing was what it seemed to be around here.

Max and Clifford came out from the crawlspace under the house and bounded around him. He figured they had retreated under there when the guns started going off. Now things were peaceful again, and they were over being scared.

He wished he was.

He put his gear in the duffle bag and looked around the furnished room to make sure he'd left nothing behind that would indicate he'd ever been there. He wished he had time to wipe down the whole room for fingerprints, but he settled for the doorknobs, the light switches, the little refrigerator, things that he had touched all the time. He heard the back door slam and went out of the room.

Dana was dressed in the usual jeans and shirt. She walked to the garage and hauled the door up. A ten-year-old pickup was inside, backed in so that it faced out. The pickup had a camper top over the bed.

"Put your stuff in the back," she told him. "It's unlocked."

While he did that, she returned to the house and came back with her suitcase in one hand and the rifle in the other.

"Both shotguns are in the kitchen," she said. "There's a bag on the table with Roy's revolver and some other handguns in it. Get all of them and put them in the back, too."

He saw that she had the little automatic tucked in the waistband of her jeans. Her shirt would cover it if she pulled out the tails.

"Shouldn't I have a gun, too?"

"You weren't in any hurry to shoot Hans when he was choking me."

"I didn't know what to do. Good Lord, I was in shock after everything that happened. Anyway, you about ruined me when you kneed me in the balls. You're lucky I can even get around."

"You're lucky I didn't kill you when you started acting so crazy." She looked like she wanted to say something else, but she stopped herself and went on, "Just get the rest of the guns, okay?"

Toby went in the house, put both shotguns under his left arm, and picked up the burlap bag full of handguns. He took them out and put them in the pickup. Dana went inside and came back with another small suitcase. She stowed it in the back, under the camper top with the guns, the other suitcase, and Toby's duffle bag.

She put her hands on her hips and said, "I guess we're ready to go. I'll pull the pickup out, and you put the cop car in there."

"You want me to drive that highway patrol car?"

"It'll be better if we don't leave it sitting in front of the house all day." She took some keys from her pocket and held them out to him.

"I didn't think you'd want to search the body, so I did it."

She was right about that, anyway. He took the keys and walked around the house toward the patrol car, casting nervous glances toward the highway as he approached the vehicle. Nobody out there on the road was paying any attention to what was going on here. Everybody drove at least seventy miles an hour on those flat Panhandle highways, and a lot of people went eighty or ninety. They would zip past the farm without ever really seeing it.

He heard noises coming from the car's radio before he even opened the door. He couldn't make sense of the chatter, so he ignored it, got in, started the engine. It wasn't any problem to drive over to the garage. Dana had the pickup pulled to one side, out of the way. Toby drove the patrol car into the garage, killed the engine, got out. He reached back in with his handkerchief to wipe the steering wheel.

"Come on," Dana called from the pickup. "Let's go."

Toby started toward her, then stopped. He pointed to the two dogs sitting beside the house, watching the goings-on with lolling tongues and interested though unaware eyes.

"What about those guys?"

"Leave them here," Dana said. "When the cops show up, they'll do something about them."

"Yeah, take them to the pound and gas them."

"You don't know that. Now get in."

Toby hesitated. Dana was starting to sound exasperated with him, and he remembered the way she had dealt with Roy and Hans.

"Sorry, guys," he said to Max and Clifford as he went to the pickup. He got in and pulled the door shut. Dana drove in front of the house and turned onto the dirt road leading to the highway.

They hadn't gone very far before Toby looked in the big mirror on his side and saw the two dogs running after them. Dana must have seen them, too, because she said, "Shit," and hit the brakes. She brought the pickup to a stop, and for a second Toby thought she might get out and shoot Max and Clifford with the automatic just to be done with them. Then she said, "All right, get them and put them in the back."

He reached for the door handle. "Okay."

A couple of minutes later they were on their way, all four of them.

3.

The speedometer needle hovered around eighty. It had been that way for quite a while. Toby watched it and finally said, "You keep driving like this, you'll get pulled over. I don't think you want that. Especially with all those guns in the back."

"You let me worry about the driving."

"Where are we going?"

"Away from that farm."

"My mother's farm."

Dana glanced over at him, taking her eyes off the road for a second.

"I guess you want to know the truth," she said.

"I'd appreciate it." Toby paused and then gave in to the impulse. "That is, if you still know how to tell it."

"Huh. You don't have any right to talk. You didn't come around looking for a job. You were looking for your mother. And when you thought you'd found her, you *slept* with her."

"I fucked her," Toby said. "She deserved it. She abandoned me."

"Maybe she had a good reason. Maybe she thought she couldn't take care of you."

"Don't make excuses for her! What do you know about it, anyway?"

She looked at him again. "Maybe more than you think."

They were both quiet again, the moment stretching out into an uncomfortable silence. Toby broke it by saying, "What happened to her, anyway?"

"She died about six months ago. Cancer. I'd been staying with her for a while, taking care of her."

"What about the rest of her family?"

Dana shook her head. "She didn't have any. Just me, and I wasn't really family." She added, "So what we did still isn't incest."

Toby let that pass. "How did you come to be there?"

"We met at the hospital in Amarillo, of all places. She was there having some tests done ... tests that didn't turn out so good ... and I was in the ER."

"Gunshot wound?"

"Don't be a smart ass. No, as a matter of fact, I had the worst case of the flu I've ever had. My fever wouldn't go down. The doctors wanted to hospitalize me, but I wouldn't let them."

"So you went home with my mom instead."

"That's right. I guess she felt sorry for me, and I think she didn't want to be alone after she got the news about her condition. Once I got better, I decided to stick around for a while and take care of her like she'd been taking care of me." She smiled. "I needed a place to lie low, anyway."

"What are you?" he asked. "Who were those guys?"

"Bank robbers." She looked at him again. "So am I."

"The way you killed those guys ... I never saw anything like it."

"It was them or me. And you. If they had gotten what they wanted, Hans and Roy wouldn't have left either of us alive."

"They wanted money," Toby said. "Four hundred grand, Hans said. Did you double-cross them or something?"

"No, somebody else did that. I just got the blame for it."

"So you don't have the money?"

"No. I got the shaft just like they did."

Toby thought about that for a while before asking, "What are you going to do now?"

"If those two found me, the others might, too. The only way to keep them from killing me is to give them what they want."

"How are you going to do that if you don't have the money?"

Dana took her right hand off the wheel for a moment, lowered it to her waist, touched the butt of the automatic.

"I have to steal it back from the person who has it."

4.

They stopped at a cinder-block motel that had been squatting beside the highway for at least forty years. The coat of ugly green paint on the exterior walls looked about that old, too. But the buzzing neon vacancy sign was lit, and another sign read PETS ALLOWED, so Dana pulled over. There was a truck stop on the other side of the highway where they could eat.

While Dana was registering, Toby found some cord in the back of the pickup and rigged makeshift leashes for Max and Clifford. He walked them on a grassy area next to the road. Dana came out of the motel office, pulled the pickup across the courtyard to park in front of one of the units. Toby led the dogs over there.

Dana unlocked the room door, carried her smaller suitcase inside along with the burlap bag containing the handguns. She left the rifle and the shotguns inside the back of the pickup. The motel wasn't very busy, but there were a few other people staying there. Toby supposed she didn't want anybody to see the long guns.

He left his duffle bag in the pickup, too, and went into the room with the dogs. The air was stifling hot and smelled of old cigarette smoke, sweat, disinfectant, and sex. Dana turned on the air conditioner. The fan rattled into life, and a second later the compressor clunked on.

She looked at him and said, "You don't have to stay with me, you know. It's safe for us to split up now. Nobody knows you were back there at the farm with me."

Toby shrugged. "I thought about it. I even thought about walking over to that truck stop to hitch a ride out of here."

"Do it. You can leave the dogs. I'll take care of them."

"All right. That's what I'll do. Take it easy." He walked out of the room, shutting the door behind him.

Just like that. It was that simple. Nothing had gone like he planned, of course. Well, almost nothing. But that was the way life was, always throwing curves at a guy.

He got his duffle bag from the pickup, threw it over his shoulder, walked to the edge of the highway. Looked back to see if Dana was watching him from the window of the motel room. She wasn't. That came as no surprise.

Traffic wasn't too heavy. Toby walked across the road and went into the restaurant area of the truck stop. He tossed the bag into an empty booth, slid in beside it on the leather-covered seat. A waitress came. He ordered coffee.

It wasn't very good, but he sat there a long time drinking it.

5.

He was sitting on the bed, picking at little pills of fabric on the spread, when Dana came out of the shower wearing a robe and drying her hair. She stopped short and looked at him.

"You already had one shower today," he said.

"I can't seem to get the smell of blood off. What are you doing here, Toby?"

"I couldn't do it. I sat over there and watched the trucks pull in and out, and I just couldn't try to get a ride. I couldn't just leave you here."

She tossed the towel through the open bathroom door onto the floor. "How did you get back in?"

"The lock on the door didn't keep me out. It sure as hell wouldn't stop a professional bank robber."

"And exactly why did you come back? I told you, it's safe enough for us to go our own ways now."

"I need to find out more about my mother. And you might need me." He pointed to the paper sack he had set down on the scarred dresser. "I brought cheeseburgers."

Dana laughed, picked up a brush, started brushing out her wet hair. "Thanks for the food, but I don't really need you, Toby. You weren't good for anything when Roy and Hans busted in."

"Hey, they took me by surprise. I expected to find my mother, not Bonnie Parker."

"How does a kid like you know who Bonnie Parker is?"

"I read sometimes. And that old movie is a classic."

She shook her head and put the brush down. "Old movie."

"Anyway, you do need me. What if I was one of the guys who are after you? You might've stepped out of the bathroom and found yourself looking down the barrel of a gun."

She reached into the pocket of the robe and pulled out the small, flat automatic.

"Yeah, could be," she said.

Toby swallowed as he looked at the gun. "You still need somebody to watch your back."

"You realize we're talking about people who would kill you without even blinking?"

"I know. But I don't want anything to happen to you."

She put the gun in her pocket and sat down on the other side of the bed. "Why? I'm not your mother, remember?"

"No, but I really like you."

"You didn't look like you liked me this morning. You looked like you wanted to strangle me."

"That's when I thought—"

"You thought I was your mother. Somehow that doesn't make me feel any better about having you around."

He swung around so that his back was to her and leaned over, putting his head in his hands.

"I was just upset. I wasn't really going to do anything. I ... I just wanted to scare her. The same way I was scared when I was a little kid and I realized my own mother didn't want me."

"It wasn't like that."

"How do you know what it was like?"

"Grace talked to me. She told me a lot about her life while ..."

"While she was dying?"

"Yes."

Toby looked around over his shoulder. "Tell me about her?"

"After we eat." Dana smiled as Max padded over to the dresser and sniffed the paper sack. "I think the dogs are getting impatient."

They sat on the bed and ate the greasy cheeseburgers, breaking off pieces of bun and meat to give to the dogs. Dana laughed as they grabbed eagerly at the food.

The atmosphere in the room was more relaxed after they had eaten. Toby said, "So tell me about her. You knew her a lot better than I ever did. I don't even remember her."

"She was a good woman. A kind-hearted woman. I think she knew I was running away from something, but she never asked any questions. She just took me in."

"And you took care of her."

"I tried. There wasn't much I could do for her except keep the farm going and see that she was as comfortable as possible. The doctors wanted her to stay in the hospital at the end, but there wasn't really anything they could do for her there, either. Prolong things for a few days, maybe a week or two. They admitted that. Grace said she'd rather be in her own home, instead of some damned hospital." Dana smiled. "That was about as rough as she ever got in her language."

"How did she ..." For a question he had thought about so much, now he wasn't sure how to ask it. "How did I ... did she say who my father ...?"

"Just some boy from where she grew up. That's all I know. When she got pregnant, she thought he would marry her. He didn't."

"So she gave me up."

Dana nodded. "She gave you up. For your own good. Her parents threw her out. She was a kid herself, she knew she couldn't take care of you. After she signed all the papers with the adoption agency, she came to Texas. She wound up marrying a man in Amarillo named Halligan. She didn't change her name to throw you off her trail."

"Yeah, I knew she was married. What happened to him?"

"He was killed in an accident on his job. He was a construction worker, and the company settled with your mother to avoid a lawsuit. They'd been in trouble before over safety issues, and they didn't want any more problems. It was a big settlement."

"So she took the money and bought that farm?"

"That's right. She'd had a lot of bad luck in her life. She wanted to sort of hide out from the world, I guess."

"And you wanted to hide out from the guys who were looking for you."

"That's right."

Toby stood up and started to pace as much as he could in the small, cramped room.

"You said she died, but I didn't find any record of that when I was looking for her. You told me you were Grace Halligan, and you told that cop the same thing."

Dana stood up, too, went to the mirror, pushed her hair back. Toby could tell she was trying not to look at him.

"Officially, she's not dead."

"Shit! You mean you didn't report it?"

"Hans and Roy and the others, they were looking for Dana Carson. Grace Halligan didn't mean anything to them. At least that's what I thought. I figured I'd be safe there."

"So when she died, what did you do? Bury her in the back yard and just take her place?"

Slowly, Dana turned around to face him.

"Yes," she said. "That's exactly what I did."

Toby shook his head and started to pace again.

"You don't owe me anything, Toby. You can see now why I think you should just leave. Go on with your life and pretend you never even met me."

"I can't do that. Not after last night. Not after we—"

"All we did was fuck. You said so yourself. I was lonely and a damned fool. You were out to hurt the woman who abandoned you. I guess we both got what we deserved."

She turned away, started toward the bathroom. He went after her, moving in to catch hold of her elbow. She turned quickly, and her other hand came up with the little automatic in it again. She pressed the muzzle of the gun under his chin.

"Let go of me." Not angry, just cold.

"No."

"I'm warning you—"

He reached up with his free hand, moving very carefully and deliberately, and closed his fingers around the gun. He pushed it away from his throat and then took it out of her hand. She didn't fight him. He tossed the gun onto the bed.

"So things didn't turn out like we expected," he said as he looked at her, only inches separating their faces. "That's no reason we shouldn't be together. We still need each other."

"You're just a kid," she said.

"I can take care of myself. I've been on my own for a while, remember?"

"I don't know ..."

He let go of her elbow and slid both arms around her waist. "I do." He brought his mouth down on hers. Dana was stiff, reluctant at first, but then she softened in his arms. Her lips opened to him. It didn't take much to get her to fall back onto the bed. Toby's hand slipped inside the robe, found her breast.

"This guy who has the money," he whispered as he lifted his mouth from hers. "Where do we find him?"

"Dallas ... The last I heard, he was in Dallas."

Four

1.

They pulled out early the next morning, before sunrise. The parking lot of the truck stop was full despite the early hour. Dana didn't want to get in a crowd, so she and Toby bought snacks and soft drinks from the machines at the motel and let that do for breakfast. They could stop later and get something better.

The landscape was much like that around the Halligan farm. Flat, cultivated fields stretching from horizon to horizon, broken up occasionally by feed lots filled with bawling cattle. Heading east as they were, Toby and Dana were in perfect position to get the full effect of the sun as it rose. The glare slapped against their eyes. Toby didn't have any sunglasses, so all he could do was lower the visor on his side and squint.

Dana drove. He offered to spell her at the wheel, but she just shook her head. He supposed she still didn't quite trust him. After everything that had happened the day before, he couldn't blame her.

Still, parts of it had been sweet. Not the blood and the being afraid he was going to die. But before all that had started, when he had believed that he'd caught up to his mother at last.

She was dead, though, and there was nothing he could do about that. What was still to come might prove to be interesting anyway.

"You really don't have to go with me, you know that," Dana said.

"Remember how, a couple of days ago after we first kissed, I kept offering to leave the farm if you wanted me to?"

"Yeah. So?"

"Now you keep telling me I don't have to go with you. I'm going with you, Dana. I'm with you all the way, as long as you want me. You might as well get that through your head."

She didn't say anything for a minute, then, "You're stubborn for a kid."

"So I've been told."

Another few minutes of silence went by before Dana asked, "If I had told you to leave—after the kiss, I mean—would you?"

He stared out the pickup window at the fields rolling past. "Probably not."

"Not until you'd had things out with your mother."

"Yeah."

She turned her head and looked at him, taking her eyes off the long, flat, straight road. "Just what the hell did you hope to accomplish, anyway? Wanting to have sex with your own mother ..." A shudder ran through her.

"Look, I figured she fucked me by abandoning me, so I'd get back at her by doing the same thing." Toby shook his head. "I don't claim it made sense. I guess, looking at it now, it's pretty damned sick. But I never really thought about it that much. I was just mad and hurt and wanted to get back at her."

Softly, Dana said, "She really was a good woman, you know. She wondered about you, a lot. She hoped your life had turned out okay."

"Why didn't she find me and find out for sure if it had?"

"She was dying. She didn't have anything to offer you. Medical bills had taken most of the money she had. There was the farm, of course, but it never made much of a profit. She worried about you. I think she was afraid if you knew about her, you'd consider her a burden."

"Maybe I would have. She still should have looked for me."

Dana said, "It's about time you learned the way the world is may not be the way you think it should be."

"Next thing, you'll be telling me there's no Santa Claus."

"Well ..."

Toby slapped the dashboard and said, "Shit! I knew it!"

2.

She agreed to switch places with him and let him drive when they got to Wichita Falls. They stopped at a pancake house for a late breakfast or early lunch, however you wanted to look at it, walked Clifford and Max, and fed them the leftovers they'd brought from the pancake house in foam containers.

"They're going to get fat, laying around in the back of the pickup all day and eating people food," Toby said.

"It won't go on forever," Dana said. "Nothing does."

When they were on the road again with Toby at the wheel, he said, "Tell me about it."

"About what?"

"The robbery. Why Roy and Hans were after you."

Dana took her time about answering, then finally said, "I suppose you've got a right to know. After all, your life is in danger, too." She paused to gather her thoughts. "It was in San Antonio, not quite three years ago. We had an inside man. Well, inside woman, really. Joyce Sanders."

"Wait a minute. There was a whole gang of you?"

"Seven, counting Joyce."

"Isn't that a lot? I thought most bank robberies were pulled off by lone bandits, or two or three at most."

"And most of them get caught, too," Dana pointed out. "We didn't plan to get caught. We *didn't* get caught. The police never found out who we were."

"Oh. Okay."

"I was the driver," Dana went on. "One of the drivers. We had another vehicle waiting in an out-of-the-way place so we could switch. Gary was the driver of that one."

"Who's Gary? What did Hans and Roy do?"

"Let me tell it my own way, all right?"

"Sure, sure. Gee, touchy."

"All right. Larry Dunaway planned the whole thing. He knew Joyce, who worked at the bank. It took him a while to convince her to go along with his idea. Once she agreed, Larry started recruiting the rest of us. Roy and Hans always worked together. I had worked with both Gary and Walt—"

"Walt?"

"Walt Brittain. Gary's last name is Mitchell. Roy was Roy Hargis, Hans was Hans Diedrichson. Got the cast of characters straight now?"

Her question was sharply put, and so was his reply. "Sure. I just want to know who might be trying to kill me before the day is over."

Dana sighed. "Like I said, Larry planned the whole thing. Joyce was the executive assistant to the president of the bank. She let us know when the most cash would be on hand. Walt and Roy went in first with guns. They had the steadiest nerves, so they were good for that part. Larry and Hans were right behind them. They had disabled the alarms by cutting the right power line a minute earlier, and Hans had a gadget that put out an electromagnetic pulse strong enough to kill all the cell phones and radios in a three or four block radius. Walt and Roy kept everybody under control while Larry and Hans took Joyce and the bank president into the vault and cleaned it out. Then they knocked out the guy and took Joyce hostage."

"So they could get her out of the bank without anybody knowing she'd been in on the robbery," Toby said.

"That's right."

"What about you?"

"I had it all timed. I drove up in the bank parking lot in an SUV, looking like a soccer mom."

"A milf," Toby said.

"A what?"

"A Mom I'd Like to Fuck. Internet porn. Being able to find sex stuff on the Internet is a required course for high school males these days. In my case, of course, milf takes on a whole new mean—"

"All right, I get it. Anyway, I get out of the SUV just as the others come out of the bank, and they run up to me and hustle me back into the SUV."

"Because you're another hostage."

"They force me to drive away. Of course, enough people see this so that the cops think they're dealing not only with a bank robbery but also with a hostage situation. But I only go a few blocks in the SUV before we all switch to a cable TV van in a parking garage. Gary drives away, and it's all over. Nobody has a clue what we've done."

"Weren't there security cameras in the parking garage?"

"Gary had already disabled them before we get there."

"And nobody thought that was suspicious?"

"Vandals go after cameras all the time. Nothing that unusual about it."

"Still, with a big bank robbery only a few blocks away, it looks like the cops would have checked out that angle."

"Maybe they did, but they didn't find anything to lead to us. Look, the plan wasn't fool-proof. No plan is. No crime is. But what counts is the result. We got away with it."

"And then ...?"

Max started to bark in the back of the pickup.

"And then the dog needed to take a crap," Dana said. "Better pull over at the next good place."

3.

When they were on the road again, Dana continued, "Larry had rented a deer lease up in the Hill Country where we could go after the job. We had four cars waiting for us there so we could go our own way after the split. There was a little cabin, a pretty crude place, no running water or electricity, but we didn't need luxury, just a place to divide the money. Larry had brought in some booze and food earlier, so we could celebrate a little before we left."

Her voice hardened as she went on, "Things didn't go too good after we got there. We started counting the money ..."

"Not as much as you thought there would be?" Toby asked.

"Joyce had told us a minimum of two million. Instead there was a little over four hundred thousand. I think it was an honest mistake. Joyce looked so surprised and so scared, and she wasn't that good an actress."

"Four hundred thousand split seven ways ... that's only something over fifty thousand apiece."

"A little over fifty-seven thousand each. Not bad for a day's work, but not enough to risk your life and freedom over. But still, there it was. Better than nothing, and better luck next time. Then it got ugly. Roy suggested that Joyce give up her share, since it was her mistake. Larry wouldn't go along with that. Roy backed down after a while, but there were hard feelings. And since Roy was mad already, he got the bright idea that he wanted something else out of the deal."

"What?"

"Me."

Toby glanced over at her, frowning.

"Walt and Gary had put away quite a bit of the booze, so they were drunk enough to go along with Roy when he said they all ought to party with me before we split up."

"You mean—?"

"Yeah, a gang-bang. I didn't go along with the idea. Larry and Joyce stayed out of it, and Hans didn't care one way or the other. Nothing about sex ever interested him. It could have gotten really bad, but then Hans passed out."

"Dead drunk?"

"That's what I thought at first. But then Roy got a funny look on his face and keeled over, too. I knew something was wrong. I would have taken advantage of the opportunity and got out of there, but the same thing hit me before I could make it to the door. I went down and out, drugged just like the others. I woke up in my car, in a roadside park a hundred miles from there. No money, of course, except a hundred bucks or so in my pocket, and not even a gun. I knew right away that Larry had done it. He brought the food and drink in."

"You think he was planning all along to rip off the rest of you?"

"Sure. I wondered for a while if he just came up with the idea when he saw there wasn't any two million, but he would have had to prepare. No, it was all planned out ahead of time. He was going for the whole two million all along."

"If you can see that, why the hell can't the others? Why come after you?"

"Because after dumping me at that park, he went back to the deer lease and doped himself just enough to knock himself out for a little while. The others all came to before he did. They were all there, I was gone, and the money was gone. He'd hidden it somewhere, of course. And the whole thing was pinned neatly on me."

Toby shook his head. "If you were unconscious, you can't be sure about all of this."

"It's the only explanation that makes sense. Larry was the only one left awake when I passed out. Earlier, he made sure that I was alone in the cabin with the food and drink. There was a chemical toilet in a closet, and he waited until I was in there and called all the others outside to look at some goddamn deer. If it hadn't been that, he would have found some other excuse. And Roy and Walt and Gary played right into his hands by being mad at me already, because I wouldn't go along with their gang-bang idea." She laughed, a low, humorless sound. "Larry's a devious son of a bitch, a good planner. But he's also lucky. Everything broke right for him."

"So you figured all this out when you woke up in the park?"

"No, not at all. I didn't have a clue what was going on at that point. All I knew was that I'd been drugged, and I didn't have the money or a gun. There was gas in the car. I drove on up the highway to a little town called Hico and stopped at a motel. You know they have a Billy the Kid museum there?"

Toby gave a little shake of his head. "What?"

"Billy the Kid. Some old man who lived there a long time ago always claimed that he was really Billy the Kid. So the town built a little museum about him. There was a brochure about it in the motel room. I didn't stop for a look, though. The others were already looking for me because Larry had convinced them I drugged them and stole the money."

"Some of them found you?"

"Gary and Walt. They knew my car, spotted it in the motel parking lot. They busted in the room in the middle of the night and accused me of stealing the money. They had been drugged, too, and passed out the same time I did. They didn't even remember me falling down, and they wouldn't let me explain. They were so mad I thought they were going to kill me right then and there."

"But you got away from them."

"They underestimated me."

Toby remembered how she had moved when Roy and Hans got into the farm house. He could understand how somebody would assume she was less dangerous than she really was.

"I got my hands on a gun and got out of there. I thought about killing both of them, but I was still pretty confused and shaken up, even a little sick from whatever drug Larry fed us. I let it go. I shouldn't have."

"Because they're still after you."

"I dodged them clear across the state, and Texas is a big place. Gary and Walt made other tries for me, and so did Hans and Roy. I never saw Larry and Joyce again. She stayed with him for a while, but then they split up. The last I heard she had hooked up with Walt and Gary."

"But she hasn't come after you?"

"That was about the time I met your mother and dropped out of sight on the farm. I know she's still out there, though. She'll find me sooner or later, and so will Walt and Gary. Hans and Roy did."

"Would they have told the others where you were?"

Dana shook her head. "Once the money disappeared, the deal was off. It was every man for himself. But Hans and Roy always worked together, and I guess Walt and Gary decided to team up, too. Maybe they all plan to double-cross each other if and when they find the money, but that doesn't have anything to do with me. I'd be dead by that point."

They fell silent for a while. Finally Toby said, "You want to take the money from Larry and give it to this Walt and Gary."

"And Joyce. She'd kill me, too, if she got the chance."

"But you'll have to steal it from Larry. He won't just hand it over to you."

"No, I don't think he will."

"Then *he'll* be after you."

Dana said, "Not if he's dead."

4.

Skyscrapers jutted up from the rolling prairie to the south as they skirted the northern edge of Fort Worth, late that afternoon. The open country was behind them. Shopping malls, car dealerships, discount stores, motels, and fast-food restaurants lined the highway that cut across into north Dallas. Toby still had the wheel, and the traffic made him a little nervous. "Where are we going?" he asked as they passed Texas Stadium.

"Right now, just to find a decent place to stop for the night. I'll have to do some thinking, figure out some things." Dana laughed again. "It's been pretty hectic. There hasn't been much time to plan. Just to stay alive."

"That's a good start," Toby said.

He pulled off the freeway while downtown Dallas was still a good seven or eight miles away. The motel was a budget one, borderline cheap without being a total dump. Dana walked the dogs while Toby unloaded the pickup, again leaving the long guns in the back as he had the night before.

He drew the curtains in the motel room tight against the lowering sun. While he waited for Dana to get back, he took Roy's revolver out of the canvas bag and held it, pointing it at the mirror over the sink and sighting over the barrel. He had never been around guns that much; the revolver felt heavy and awkward. As he held it, though, the grips got more comfortable in his hand. He seemed to sense power flowing from it into him, more power than he had felt in quite a while. A man with a gun was never alone.

He turned and slipped the revolver back into the bag as he heard the doorknob rattle and then turn. Dana came in with Max and Clifford. The dogs were excited. After being cooped up most of the day, a brief walk wasn't enough to take care of their excess energy. Dana looked tired and frazzled.

"You may have to take them out again in a little while," she said as she closed the door and let go of the rope leashes.

"Sure, I don't mind." Toby patted his thigh, and both dogs scrambled over to him to be petted. He sat down on the edge of the queen-size bed and rubbed their ears.

"We ought to get some real leashes and halters, too."

"There's a Wal-Mart just down the service road. I'll walk down there and get whatever you want," Toby said.

"All right. We'll need some food, maybe some Cokes."

"Better make a list, so I won't forget anything."

Dana used the pad and pencil on the table to make the list, asking Toby what he liked as she wrote things down. Toby sat on the bed and watched her and petted the dogs.

"What about cookies?"

"Chocolate chip. They're my favorite."

"Fritos?"

Toby shook his head. "Barbecue potato chips."

"Dr Pepper?"

He made a face.

"I forgot, you're from Oklahoma," Dana said with a smile. "Coke, then."

"Sure, that's fine."

"No Coke, Pepsi," she said, putting a strange accent in her voice.

"What?"

This time she laughed outright. "Before your time, junior."

The hand that was rubbing Clifford's ear tightened. The little dog let out a pained yelp. Dana looked up in surprise, but the look was gone from Toby's face by then.

"What's wrong?"

"I don't know. I was just petting him. He must have a sore place somewhere, and I guess I poked it accidentally."

"Well, he looks okay now."

It was true. With the instant forgiveness of his kind, Clifford was slobbering on Toby's hand again. Toby pretended to look for the sore place on the dog's ear, but of course he didn't find it.

Dana went back to making the grocery list, and Toby said quietly to the dog, "That's a good boy, that's a good boy. I'm sorry I hurt you, Clifford. That's a good boy."

5.

Toby spent an hour walking the aisles of Wal-Mart, trying to get around old ladies who parked their cart next to one shelf and then stood beside it studying the other shelf, taking up nearly all the room. He waited patiently for them to move, leaning on the handle of his own cart. One or two of them gave him a grudging, "Sorry," as he passed, and he always said cheerfully, "No problem."

There were quite a few young mothers in the store, too, and he looked at them in appreciation of their wholesome beauty. Their kids were lucky. They got to be around them all the time.

He had half a dozen bags when he left, three dangling from each hand. He walked back along the service road to the motel and went to the door of the room and kicked it lightly. Dana opened it for him.

He'd bought sandwiches and salads in the deli for them, so they had those for supper and didn't have to go out. The room had cable TV. Even the most rundown motels had cable TV, Toby thought, already forgetting about the place they had stayed the previous night, which had had no TV at all. He watched MTV for a while, but Dana wanted to see the local news, so they switched over.

The story about the dead highway patrolman and the other two corpses being found on the farm house came up in the second segment. Even though the killings had taken place several hundred miles away, the crime was grisly enough that all the TV stations in the state were probably covering it. And there was the added attraction of a missing and presumed kidnapped woman. Grace Halligan was known to have been ill, and the sober-faced newsman didn't sound as if the authorities held out much hope for her. Their theory was that she had been taken by whoever had killed the cop and the other two men, who were so far unidentified.

"That's a lie," Dana said. "Roy did time in Iowa. They're bound to know who he is by now."

"What about Hans?"

"I don't think he was ever arrested in this country. I don't know about Germany. If he doesn't have a record there, they may never identify him."

"He didn't have a passport or any other papers?"

Dana laughed and shook her head. "Not a real one."

The newsman went on to repeat the police theory that the highway patrolman had interrupted a home invasion and robbery and gotten killed for his trouble. Speculation was that the two unidentified men were members of the gang and had been killed by their companions after some sort of falling out. The tone of the report managed to be both breathless and somber at the same time. Toby wanted to laugh at how far from the truth all of it was.

"You're right," he said. "The cops can't figure out anything."

"They didn't say anything about Dana Carson. Right now, that's all I care about."

"You think they'll dig up the back yard and find ..." Toby had to stop before he said *my mother's grave.* The whole idea was just too strange for him. For years he had held on to the belief that she was alive and that he would find her.

Dana knew what he meant. "There's no reason for them to go digging around back there," she said. "They think Grace was kidnapped. They'll look for her body, but not there on the farm."

"Yeah, I guess you're right. You should be safe from the cops, anyway."

Dana let him change the channel back to the music videos. Later, Toby walked the dogs again, using their new leashes and halters this time. By the time he got back to the room, she had already showered and was sitting up in bed wearing a light blue, sleeveless gown. She had the pad and pen and used them to scribble notes as she frowned in thought. He knew she was trying to work out what they would do next, so he kept quiet and didn't bother her. He took a shower, came out of the bathroom wearing clean underwear, and slipped into the bed beside her as she chewed on the pen. She didn't look at him as he rolled onto his side, facing away from her, and closed his eyes.

He fell asleep, so he didn't know what time it was when she finally turned out the light.

Five

1.

"How do you know Larry's here in Dallas?" Toby asked the next morning over the fast-food breakfast he had brought back to the motel room.

"I don't, not for sure. He was here the last I heard."

"Then he could be hundreds of miles away. He could even be dead."

Dana shrugged. "It's possible. If that's the case, you'd better take off and pretend you've never heard of me. I'll take my chances with Walt and Gary and Joyce."

"I'm not going to run out on you," Toby said. "You ought to know that by now."

"It's not a matter of running out on anybody. It's a matter of having some common sense."

"Nobody ever accused me of that."

She shook her head. "My hunch is that Larry's still around here somewhere. He had that four hundred thousand from the bank job. That's enough so that he could just lie low for a while. For that matter, it's enough he could have invested it and gone straight."

"You think he might have done that?"

Dana thought about it for a moment and then shook her head again. "No. Not Larry Dunaway. He always had to be planning something, working on something. Never satisfied. Even if he'd gotten the whole two million like he wanted, by this time he'd have something else in the works."

"So how do we find him?"

"I start by making a phone call. Not from here, though."

"There are pay phones down in front of Wal-Mart."

Dana nodded. "Then that's where we'll go."

They finished eating. The day before, Toby had bought cans of dog food with lids that peeled off. He opened one for Clifford and a couple for Max and dumped them in leftover foam containers from breakfast. The dogs ate as if they were half-starved, as usual, and when they were done he took them out for their walk.

When they got back, Dana was watching TV. "Nothing new on what happened on the farm," she said.

"If the cops were looking for us, they wouldn't put it on TV, would they?" Toby asked as he unhooked the leashes from the dogs. Max jumped onto the bed beside Dana.

She put her arm around the dog's neck. "No, probably not."

"They're bound to have found your fingerprints all over the house."

Dana nodded. "Yes."

"So, won't they be able to match them up and find out who you are?"

"I've never been arrested, Toby," she said. "Have you?"

"Me? No. Never."

"You're sure?"

He frowned. "I think I'd know about that, don't you?"

"Of course. I'm sorry. It's just that there's so much to think about, so much to keep track of. So many things that can go wrong." She hugged Max harder.

"Yeah, I know. It's okay. The cops will know we were there, but they won't know who we are."

"That's the way I have it figured," Dana said.

"How about that phone call you wanted to make?"

"It's too early. The guy won't be awake yet, and he won't like it if I wake him. I'll call him this afternoon."

"That means we've got a few hours to kill." Toby sat on the bed behind Dana and put his hands on her shoulders. As he started to rub them, he said, "Do you have any suggestions what we might do to occupy our time until then?"

Dana leaned back against him, and from the low noise of pleasure she made in her throat, he knew she had closed her eyes and was smiling. "I don't know," she said. "What do you want to do?"

He moved his hands down to her waist, slid his arms around her, and brought them up under her shirt. She wasn't wearing a bra. He filled his hands with her breasts and rubbed her hardening nipples as he leaned over and kissed her neck.

Dana pushed Max off the bed. "Down, boy."

Toby said, "Okay," as he slid one hand down over her belly and into the waistband of her jeans.

Dana laughed and turned around on the bed so that she could put her arms around Toby's neck and kiss him. She leaned back, pulling him with her.

A few moments of hurried fumbling got her jeans off and his down around his ankles. He penetrated her and started driving hard into her.

Her arms tightened around his neck. Her head tossed from side to side. She came first, and then he followed a moment later.

He was still on top of her and she was stroking his hair when she whispered, "Toby, you weren't thinking of ... you didn't think that I was ..."

"No," he said. "The thought never entered my mind."

2.

At twelve-thirty in the afternoon, they put the dogs in the back of the pickup and drove down the service road to Wal-Mart. Toby wanted to listen in on the phone call, and he and Dana both felt it wouldn't be a good idea to leave Max and Clifford alone in the motel room. They didn't want to do anything to draw attention to themselves, and if the dogs started barking or trashed the room, that could do it.

"Mr. Martinez?" Dana said into the phone. "This is Shelley, calling about the computer upgrade?"

Codes and passwords. It seemed kind of silly, but he supposed given the line of work that Dana was in, such precautions were necessary.

"Yes, it's me, Hector," Dana said. "No, really ... I'm not dead ... It's good to hear your voice, too ... I can't really discuss that ... Yes, I'd like to get together so we can talk about an old friend of ours ... That's the one. When would be a good time?"

She nodded as if the man she was talking to could see her.

"All right. Where? ... Where did you say? ... All right. I'll be there ... Alone, yes, of course."

Toby frowned. He wasn't sure who this Hector was, but it was a pretty safe bet that he was a criminal of some sort. And if Hector wanted to meet Dana alone, Toby wasn't sure if that was a good idea, either.

"Thank you, Hector," she said, and then hung up the phone.

"This is the guy you think knows where—?"

She held up a hand, palm toward him. "In the pickup."

Toby got behind the wheel out of habit now. "Where to?"

"Just drive around while we talk. Take Mockingbird and work your way east."

Toby didn't know where Mockingbird was, but when he got to the next intersection, he saw that it was the cross-street. He turned left under the freeway.

"Listen, Dana, I don't know if it's a good idea for you to be meeting this guy by yourself—"

"I'm not going to. He doesn't really expect that. He knows I'll have somebody covering me. So will he. But when we sit down to talk, it'll be just the two of us."

"I hope he picked some public place."

Dana smiled. "Listen, Hector doesn't trust me any more than I trust him. Neither of us wants to walk into a trap. He told me to meet him in the coffee shop at one of those big chain bookstores in North Dallas. I don't think any trouble is going to break out there."

Toby wasn't quite that confident, but he let it pass. "When?"

"Four o'clock this afternoon."

"Who is this guy?"

"Hector Evans is his name."

"Not Martinez?"

"No. That name and the name I used, Shelley, told him who I really am. If he had been in a situation where he couldn't talk, he would have told me I had the wrong number and hung up. But he was alone and the line was secure, so it was okay."

"Is he another bank robber?"

Dana laughed. "No, I can't imagine Hector robbing a bank. He's more into fraud, money laundering, things like that. Sometimes he brokers a deal for some arms, but that's rare. But he knows everyone in the business and keeps up to date with what's going on. He thought I was dead."

"And that's good?"

"Very good," Dana said with a nod. "It means he didn't send Roy and Hans after me. If he was telling the truth, and I think he was." She paused. "I hope he was."

Toby was silent for a moment as he thought it over. Then he said, "If there's a price on your head, what's to stop this Hector from selling you out to the other guys who are looking for you?"

"Not a thing. That's where trust comes in."

"I thought you said you didn't trust him."

"I don't, not entirely. But he's the most likely person to tell me where Larry is, so I have to trust him to a certain extent. It's all right to be suspicious of everybody, but sometimes you have to believe somebody and just hope for the best."

"All right, I guess. So you think he'll know where to find Larry?"

"I hope so. I know he's been in touch with him, because he knew about the job in San Antonio. He probably believes I stole all the money. That's the story that Larry will have put out to anybody who would listen."

"This Larry's a son of a bitch," Toby said.

"Yes, but a dangerous son of a bitch. Don't ever forget that."

"Not likely."

Dana reached over and touched his knee as he drove. "No, I mean it, Toby," she said. "Roy and Hans were bad enough. Gary and Walt are the same way. But Larry ... Larry is the most dangerous man I've ever seen."

"And yet you're planning to take that money away from him and kill him."

"Well ... I'm dangerous, too." She added with a smile, "Don't say I never warned you."

3.

They ate lunch at a restaurant beside one of the freeways that sliced through Dallas. Toby was glad Dana knew her way around the town. He would have been completely lost by now if he had been on his own. He wasn't sure he could have even found his way back to the motel.

They stopped at a small park and let the dogs run around for a while, but it was too hot to stay outside for long. The sun beat down on the asphalt and concrete, and the heat rose in waves. When they got back in the pickup, Toby turned the air conditioning vent where it blew right on him.

Following Dana's directions, he drove toward the bookstore where she would meet with Hector Evans. He dropped her off a couple of blocks away and then drove on, parking in the lot and walking into the bookstore. The magazine section was right beside the coffee shop, Dana had told him, and he saw that she was right. He would browse there while she was talking to Hector.

He tried not to look around too much. He pretended to concentrate on the magazines instead. Dropping Dana off like that worried him. If Hector had called Larry and tipped him off that Dana was in Dallas, she could walk into a trap outside the store. Or maybe Gary and Walt were in town, too, and Hector sold Dana out to them. Anything was possible.

He saw her walk past on the sidewalk just outside the store, her hair bright in the afternoon sunlight. It was a little easier then to pretend to be looking at an astronomy magazine.

The coffee shop, though open to the rest of the bookstore, had a separate entrance, too. Dana came in that door, went to the counter, ordered a cup of coffee, carried it over to a table and sat down. Toby had already been looking over the other customers, trying to pick out Hector without being too obvious about it. He didn't see anybody who seemed right. Most of the other customers were young, and many of them were female.

Dana sipped her coffee and looked at a newspaper that had been lying on the table. Fifteen minutes went by. People came in and out of the coffee shop. Toby began to wonder how long he could stand there looking at magazines. But several of the people who had been browsing when he entered the bookstore were still there, so he figured he didn't look any more conspicuous than they did.

A short, stocky man with an old-fashioned crew cut came through the bookstore into the coffee shop. He ordered coffee, and when he turned away from the counter his gaze passed right over Dana, then stopped and came back to her. He started toward her with a smile on his face.

"Hi, Shelley," he said as he came up to the table.

Dana looked up from the newspaper and smiled. "John, how are you?"

"Oh, fine, fine. How about you?"

"Okay. How's Brenda?"

"Doing all right. Staying busy all the time, as usual."

"What about the girls?"

The man rolled his eyes and laughed. "That's why Brenda's so busy, keeping up with those two."

Dana laughed, too, and then said, "Why don't you sit down for a minute? It's been ages since we've seen you and Bren."

Toby wondered if people ever really talked like that when they weren't trying to pretend to be somebody they weren't. Some of them probably did. If he ever sounded like that for real, it would be time to blow his brains out.

The man, who had to be Hector, sat down and continued exchanging small talk with Dana. Their voices gradually got lower until Toby could no longer make out what they were saying. Neither could anyone else, because nobody was sitting at a table close to them. From time to time Dana or the man laughed. His voice rose a little, and Toby caught something about cheerleading practice. Dana smiled and nodded.

Toby bit his lip and forced his eyes back to the magazine in his hands. He didn't know whether he wanted to laugh or puke, or maybe both.

Finally, Hector stood up. He said, "It was great seeing you again. Say hello to Phil for me."

"I will. And say hello to Brenda for me."

"Sure." Hector drained the last of the coffee in his cup and tossed it in a wastebasket. He strolled back into the bookstore, passing fairly close to Toby, who ignored him.

Toby waited ten minutes, then bought a magazine and left the store. He got in the pickup and drove away, going two blocks and then pulling into the parking lot of a men's clothing store. He had waited there only a few minutes when Dana opened the passenger door and climbed into the pickup.

"He's here," she said. "Larry's still in Dallas, just like I thought. And now I know where to find him."

4.

Dana laid it all out when they got back to the motel.

"The word is that I double-crossed the others and stole the money. Larry's been spreading that rumor ever since it happened, just like I thought. But after I dropped out of sight on the farm, people started to wonder if I was dead. Somebody who knew me saw me at the hospital in Amarillo, though, and finally sold the information to Roy and Hans."

"Who?" Toby said. "Who sold you out?"

Dana shook her head. "I don't know, and I don't care. What's done is done."

"You don't want to pay them back for what they did?"

"Payback is the most overrated commodity in the world. It doesn't change a fucking thing."

"But it's justice," Toby said.

"No, it's revenge. Maybe it makes you feel better. Some people might brood over something so much and for so long that they can't function anymore. Then it might make sense to go ahead and try to get your revenge. But it still doesn't change a single thing in the past."

Toby couldn't argue with that. He shrugged and said, "Okay, you're willing to let that go. But you want to find Larry to get even with him for what he did."

Again, Dana shook her head. "No, I just want the money so I can put a stop to people trying to kill me. It's as simple as that."

He couldn't let it go. "And you won't feel the least bit of satisfaction when you blow Larry's head off?"

"Not really. We worked together with no problems on several other jobs. Then he got greedy."

Toby grunted. "End of story?"

"End of story."

"So where is he now?"

"He has an apartment here in town, and he hangs out at a club in Deep Ellum."

"Is he into anything crooked?"

"Hector didn't know about it if he is, and since Hector knows just about everything ..."

"What's he been doing, then, for the past two years?"

"Lying low, like I said."

"By hanging out at nightclubs?"

"Larry always liked the nightlife. But Deep Ellum is a popular place. There are always crowds. You'd be amazed how low a profile you can keep in a mob of people. Sometimes that's actually easier."

Toby nodded. "Yeah, I guess that makes sense. So what do we do now?"

"We have to get close to him first. I guess that means some club-hopping."

"Isn't he liable to shoot you on sight? He knows what he did to you."

Dana smiled. "But he doesn't know that I know."

"What?" Toby asked, frowning. He didn't like the way she always seemed to be thinking two steps ahead of him.

"I didn't let on to Hector that I suspect Larry of the double-cross. In fact, I made it sound like I'm looking for Larry so I can ask him to help me."

"To help you?"

"That's right. As far as Hector knows, I think Walt or Gary or even Joyce pulled the double-cross. Maybe all three of them were in it together. Maybe Joyce planned the whole thing. After all, she left Larry not long after that and hooked up with Gary and Walt."

"But they're looking for you to try to get the money back. Why would they do that if they had the money all along?"

"I don't believe they really do, of course. This job has Larry's fingerprints all over it. But if they *were* responsible for the double-cross, what better way of throwing suspicion off themselves than to pretend to be after me?"

Toby put his hands on his head. "They really *are* after you, at least according to what you told me before."

"Sure they are, because they fell for Larry's trick. But what I'm trying to do is make Larry believe that I don't suspect him of what I know he really did. That way he won't try to kill me as soon as I get in touch with him."

"But how will he know you don't suspect him?"

"Hector will tell him. At least, that's what I'm counting on."

"Why would he do that?"

"Hector tries to stay in good with as many people as possible. If he thought I wanted to kill Larry, he would have to make a decision: keep my trust, or sell me out to Larry. Either way, he runs the risk of making a bad enemy. But if he thinks I want Larry to help me, then he can tip off Larry and do a favor for both of us by smoothing the way. You see?"

Toby took a deep breath. "In other words, you don't trust anybody, you never tell the truth, and you manipulate and use people every way you possibly can."

"That's it. You've got it," Dana said.

"What about me?"

"What about you?"

"Are you lying to me, manipulating me? Do you not trust me, either?"

Her voice softened. "Like I said, sooner or later you've got to trust somebody. I guess that makes you my leap of faith, Toby."

5.

The area of downtown Dallas known as Deep Ellum was full of night-clubs. Music of every kind, from country to hip-hop, from techno to *Tejano*, drifted out onto the crowded sidewalks. Most of the people were young and well-dressed. They either made good money or were able to keep up the pretense that they did. Toby had never seen anything like it in suburban Oklahoma City.

Dana was older than most of the people they passed on the sidewalks, but with her blond hair and unlined skin she looked younger than she really was. She wore a blue dress that was short to start with and had a slit on one side that revealed even more thigh. She had the legs to carry it off, too. Compared to him, she looked not all that much older and definitely hipper.

The club they were looking for was called *Pasqual*. Dana had no trouble finding it. She seemed to have a built-in talent for locating places. A doorman let them in. He gave Dana a big smile and barely glanced at Toby. Toby figured that since he was with Dana, the doorman assumed he was older than he really was. It would have been embarrassing to get carded and refused admission to the club, not to mention dangerous, since he wasn't going to let Dana get anywhere near Larry unless he was somewhere close by, too.

Dance music pounded at them. Some parts of the club were dimly lit while others were illuminated by bright spotlights. Dancers writhed in the glare. The noise level was high as people tried to talk and laugh over the music. Everybody had a drink. The bathrooms were probably full of people snorting cocaine. Toby frowned. This wasn't his kind of place.

Dana got beers for them at the bar and led the way to a tiny table tucked in an alcove. They sat down, sipped the beers, studied the dancers and the other people in the club.

"I don't see him," Dana said after a few minutes.

"You're sure this is the right place?"

"Hector said Larry comes here almost every night."

Toby worried a little because they had to raise their voices to be heard, even though they sat so close beside each other that their legs touched. But if it was that hard for him to hear what Dana said, it would be impossible for anybody else to eavesdrop.

"You want to dance?" he asked after a few minutes.

Dana laughed and shook her head. "I can pull off the look, but if I get out there on the dance floor people are going to know I'm not young enough to be here."

"That's bullshit. I never saw anybody who can move like you do."

"Only under certain circumstances," she said, and he knew what she meant.

With a gun in her hand, while somebody was trying to kill her ...

They nursed the beers and waited, and Toby knew by the way Dana's leg stiffened where it was pressed against his when she saw the man they were looking for. He followed her gaze.

The man was thin and probably looked a little taller than he really was because of his gangling build. He had thinning brown hair, a ready smile that he flashed at nearly every woman he passed, and a little tuft of hair under his bottom lip. He was too old for this crowd, but the beautiful redhead on his arm was no more than nineteen. Toby hated him on sight.

Dana let him get nearly to the table before she stood up and stepped smoothly in front of him. "Hello, Larry," she said.

Six

1.

He didn't look surprised, so Toby knew that Hector must have told him about the meeting with Dana that afternoon.

"Dana! How are you? It's been a long time."

Larry grinned at her as he spoke. He took her right hand in both of his, which meant he had to disengage his arm from the redhead's. She didn't look happy about that.

"Why don't you sit down and join us?" Dana said.

Before Larry could answer, the redhead said, "I don't want to sit down. I came to dance, Larry."

"So go and dance," he told her. "I'll catch up to you later."

"But I want to dance with *you!*"

"Go," he told her, and Toby heard the steel in his voice. So did the redhead, because she went. But not without casting a resentful glare over her shoulder. It was funny, but she was a lot closer to Toby's age, the sort of girl he would have wanted for his girlfriend at one time. Not anymore, of course. Not after the past few weeks.

Larry looked at him and asked Dana, "Who's your friend?"

"Toby," she said.

"That's a dog's name." He flashed that grin again. "No offense, Toby, my man."

"Sure," Toby said. He hated the son of a bitch already, so it didn't matter.

"Toby's with me," Dana said.

Larry nodded. "Good enough for me. Let's sit down." He motioned to the bartender, and a waitress brought over a drink by the time the three of them were sitting down.

Larry picked up the glass and swallowed some of the liquor. He leaned back in his chair, looked out at the closest section of brightly lit dance floor, and smiled as his date went past, dancing so enthusiastically that her waist-length red hair swung out well away from her body. The man dancing with her was almost drooling.

"Dumb as a rock, of course," Larry said. His voice had a slight twang to it that wasn't quite Texan. Arkansas or Louisiana, maybe. "I wouldn't put up with her if she wasn't such a good fuck." He looked away from the redhead and toward Dana. "Now, what about you?"

"I'm a good fuck, too," she said.

Larry laughed. "Yeah, I bet I could ask old Toby here about that."

Toby leaned forward in his chair. "Listen—"

Dana stopped him with a small motion of her hand. Larry laughed again and said, "Hell, son, I'm just screwin' with you. Don't take it serious. Dana and me go way back. She knows how I think and I know how she thinks."

"Are you sure of that, Larry?" she said.

"Well, I hope so, because if I'm wrong, there's sure liable to be some trouble."

"No trouble," she said with a shake of her head. "I'm here because I need your help."

"My help? What in the world could I help you with, darlin'?"

"You can help me keep the others from killing me."

"Over that money you stole after the bank job in San Antonio? I ought to hold a grudge against you myself about that, but I'm such a forgiving old bastard I can't bring myself to do it."

"I *didn't* steal the money. You've got to believe me, Larry. I never saw that money again."

"But it must've been you. All the rest of us were knocked out, and when we woke up, you and the money were gone."

Nothing was real to these people. They told their lies so often that a lie and the truth were the same thing to them. Just words that came out of the mouth and meant nothing, or everything, depending on what you wanted them to mean.

"I was drugged, too," Dana said. "You've got to believe me, Larry. I didn't have anything to do with stealing the money."

Larry tossed off the rest of his drink. "All the rumors I've heard say that you did."

He didn't mention that he had been the source of those rumors.

"I've heard the same thing. That's why I've been on the run the past couple of years. I knew the rest of you wouldn't believe me. But I've got to trust somebody again … I've got to have help …"

Just the faintest tremor in her voice. Just enough to remind a man that although she was a tough, deadly woman, she was still a woman and needed a man.

Lord, she was good.

"Listen here now," Larry said. "You mean to tell me you really didn't double-cross us and take that money?"

"I really didn't. I swear it."

He looked baffled. "Then ... who did?"

It was a good act, but it *was* an act. Toby was certain of it.

"I think it was Joyce," Dana said.

Larry stared at her. "No, it couldn't be. Joyce was never that smart."

"She left you not long after that, didn't she? I heard that she was with Walt and Gary now. They've been looking for me, I think. She told them that I stole the money, but it was her all along. She has it hidden somewhere, so that no one will ever suspect her."

"That's crazy! But ..."

Larry hesitated, and Toby knew he was at least nibbling at the bait.

Dana set the hook. "You're the only one I was sure of. I know you didn't do it."

Toby hoped she hadn't jerked too hard with that. Larry stared at her for a long moment. "How come you know that?"

She smiled. "Because you know I'd come after you and kill you if you ever tried a stunt like that."

A laugh burst from him. "Well, hell, that's true enough! You always did have a temper. I'm still having a hard time wrapping my old brain around all this, though."

"Maybe it wasn't Joyce," Dana said. "Maybe it was one of the others. Whoever it was, they stashed the money and set me up to take the blame for the double-cross. They're waiting for the others to catch up to me and kill me. Then, when the money isn't found, they figure everyone will assume I hid it somewhere and it's gone for good now. They let a little time pass, separate themselves from whoever they're with, grab the money, and vanish forever to Mexico or Europe. Simple."

"On four hundred grand?" Larry shook his head. "Not enough money to vanish forever."

"That depends on how rich you want to live. Maybe whoever pulled the double-cross is more interested in living than in living rich."

Larry frowned like he couldn't understand that concept, but after a moment, he nodded. "Everything you say makes sense, Dana ... but only if I start by believing that you didn't steal the money from the rest of us."

"That's what I'm asking you to believe. Because it's true."

Toby kept his expression tightly under control. Larry was too good to reveal his thoughts on his face, but Toby knew what he had to be thinking: he was in the clear. Dana blamed one of the others for the double-cross. She wasn't coming after him.

"What do you want me to do?" he asked. "How can I help you?"

"Is there someplace else we can talk, some place quieter?"

"Sure, we can go back to my apartment. Kelly won't like it, but screw her. In fact, if you want to kill a little time, Toby, you might just want to look into that possibility."

2.

Larry's apartment was on the edge of Highland Park, just over the line in the Dallas city limits, not far from SMU. It was a two-story duplex. According to him, the other side was occupied by a stockbroker and his lawyer wife, who were both in Cancun at the moment.

"So we don't have to worry about how much noise we make," he'd said before they left the club.

That didn't sound too promising to Toby. He didn't see any reason for them to make much noise. Unless guns started going off, and he didn't want to think about that.

Dana had the small pistol in her purse. While they were in the pickup following Larry and the redhead over here, Toby put a revolver in his pants pocket. It was the one that had been taped under the desk in the living room back at the farm house—the gun that had killed Roy Hargis—and it was compact enough so that it didn't make a big bulge in Toby's pocket.

"Don't use it unless you have to," Dana told him.

"How will I know?"

"If Larry is about to kill one of us ... don't let him."

Toby made a face. "Not all of us are hardened criminals, you know. This stuff is all new to me."

Dana sighed and said, "I wish you'd never had to learn any of it."

Toby wouldn't go so far as to say that. Sure, he had been terrified part of the time, and when he wasn't out-and-out scared he was still nervous. But it was exciting, too. Most people never experienced the same level of excitement as he had recently. Maybe they were lucky that was true; maybe not.

"Looks like we're here," Dana said as she parked behind Larry's Lexus in a driveway that ran beside the duplex. "Let's hope the cops don't ticket us for having too unpretentious a vehicle."

Actually, that was a worry. The pickup, after all, belonged to Grace Halligan, and weren't the cops looking for Grace, thinking that she was a kidnap victim?

He stopped Dana with a hand on her arm before they got out of the pickup. "What about the license plates? Isn't the pickup registered to my mother?"

Dana just looked at him. "I've changed the plates three times since we left the farm."

There she was, two steps ahead of him again. "When?"

"I swiped some off other pickups while you were walking the dogs that first night."

"Oh."

He had a lot to learn, all right. If he lived long enough.

Larry took them inside. The redhead, Kelly, was pouting. Larry swatted her on the ass and said, "Go upstairs and watch TV. The grownups have to talk business."

She pointed at Toby. "He's not much older than I am!"

"Well, if he gets cranky, we'll send him upstairs, too."

Kelly slid over against Toby, leaning into him and licking his earlobe. "If you get bored, I'll be in the room at the top of the stairs." The warm roundness of her left breast pressed against his arm.

"Thanks, I'll remember that."

She seemed disappointed in his reaction. She went up the stairs. Larry ushered Dana and Toby into a den. Like the rest of the apartment, it had thick carpet on the floor and was expensively furnished. A giant-screen TV angled across one corner of the room, flanked by a massive stereo system. The opposite corner was taken up by a massive, highly polished desk with a computer on it.

Larry went to a bar to fix drinks. Toby asked for a beer, Dana for scotch and soda. Larry did the honors, then said, "Now, you were going to tell me what I can do to help you, Dana."

"Do you know how to get in touch with the others?"

"You mean Gary and Walt and Joyce?"

"And Hans and Roy. I imagine they're still after me, too."

"You haven't heard?"

"Heard what?"

Larry sipped his drink. "Roy and Hans are dead."

Dana just stared levelly at him. "No, I hadn't heard. But I can't say that I'm sorry. What happened to them? A job that went wrong?"

"They were killed out in West Texas just a few days ago. Under mysterious circumstances, as the old saying goes."

Dana shook her head. "I hadn't heard anything about it. But all it really means to me is that there are two less people in the world who represent a threat. That just leaves the other three. Can you get in touch with them?" she asked again.

Larry wiggled a hand back and forth. "Maybe. You know there are always mechanisms for that. Sometimes they don't work, though."

"I want you to talk to them, tell them I didn't betray them. And that I don't have the money and never did."

"One of them must already know that."

Dana nodded. "The one who planned the double-cross."

"Even if I intercede on your behalf, he or she won't let the other two be convinced. The blame has to stay on you until you're dead."

"I know that. I want to plant the seed, though. I want them to start thinking that maybe, just maybe, it wasn't me."

"I'll do what I can," Larry said with a shrug. "I can't guarantee anything, though."

"I know that. I just appreciate anything you can do—"

A crash sounded from upstairs, and a second later, the redhead screamed.

3.

Larry swung toward the stairs, and by the time he was turned around, he had a gun in his hand. Dana had taken the little automatic from her purse, too. Toby reached for the revolver, but the hammer snagged on his pocket as he tried to pull it out. He heard cloth rip as he tugged harder. The gun came free.

"Cover the door," Dana said to him.

He turned to face the door to the foyer, holding the revolver in both hands. Fear and excitement went through him, mingling in his veins. He realized that he wasn't afraid of dying; not much, anyway. But he wondered how he would do if it came down to shooting. He wanted to hold up his end.

"Take it easy down there," a man's voice called from upstairs. "Take it easy and nobody gets hurt."

"Chuck?" Larry said.

Toby knew he shouldn't look around, knew he ought to keep his attention on the door like Dana had told him, but he couldn't resist taking a glance over his shoulder. He saw the redhead's nylon-clad legs coming down the stairs, followed closely by a pair of legs in trousers. The rest of the redhead came into view. A man stood behind her, an arm looped around her neck. The man's other hand held a pistol with the barrel pressed against Kelly's head. It looked sort of odd, the way the barrel disappeared into that thick mass of copper-colored hair.

Two more men followed them down the stairs. They had guns, too, and they covered Dana and Larry while Dana and Larry covered them. Toby supposed he was the wild card here.

"Toby, don't move," Dana said quietly. She must have been thinking the same thing.

"We didn't know you were going to have company, Larry, or we would have called first." That came from the man holding the gun on the redhead.

"Yeah, I'll bet," Larry said. "What do you want, Chuck?"

"What do you think? There's a little matter of a hundred and fifty grand you need to clear up."

"I told you you'd get paid."

"You told me that over a week ago, and so far I haven't seen shit from you. I want my money, Larry."

A hundred and fifty thousand dollars. Larry ought to have that much. He had taken four hundred thousand from Dana and the others. That was a big chunk of the money Dana hoped to recover, but Larry might not have any choice except to use it.

"Why are you doing this? You know I'm good for it. Haven't I always paid you in the past?"

"You never owed this much for this long," Chuck said. He was middle-aged and mostly bald with a fringe of gray hair around his ears and the back of his head. He didn't look all that dangerous. But he seemed to enjoy it when he ground the gun barrel against Kelly's head hard enough to make her cry out in pain. "Give me the money, Larry, or things are going to get a whole lot worse."

"What are you going to do, shoot that cunt? You do, and I'll put a bullet through your head before you get through pulling the trigger."

"My boys will kill you."

"And Dana and Toby will kill them."

Dana said, "If you can guarantee that Toby and I are the only ones who walk away alive, hell, let's get this started, Larry."

Chuck frowned at her and then gave an abrupt bark of laughter. "Dana," he said. "Dana Carson?"

"That's right," she said.

"I thought you were dead."

"Not until I'm in the ground ... and maybe not then."

And this was the woman Toby had believed was his mom. He should have been so lucky.

"All right, I'm willing to talk about this," Chuck said.

"Let Kelly go?" Larry said.

"No, not yet. If nothing else, built like she is with those big tits, she makes a good shield."

Larry nodded. "Big tits always come in handy."

"Hey," Dana said. "I could take offense at a remark like that."

"Sorry, darlin'. Your tits are perfectly fine from what I've seen of them, which you got to remember ain't a whole hell of a lot."

They were all crazy, joking about tits at a time like this. Or maybe that was how they kept from going crazy.

"One hundred and fifty grand," Chuck said. "You've either got it or you don't."

"I don't have it *on* me," Larry said. "But I can put my hands on that much in a day or two."

"You've had a week. Why haven't you gotten it before now?"

"I've been busy."

"Screwing around is what you've been. Trying to test my patience."

"No, I swear it, Chuck. I'll get your damn money. I just need a little more time."

Chuck frowned as he thought it over. Toby risked a glance at the other two men. They were big, hard-faced, dead-eyed. Shoot or don't shoot, it didn't matter to them. He tried to assume something of the same look himself, but he figured the attempt was a miserable failure.

Even though, truth to tell, he didn't really care. His world had been turned upside-down anyway, these past few weeks.

"All right," Chuck said after a few moments that seemed longer. "I'll be generous. I'll give you forty-eight hours."

"I'll have the money. You wait and see."

Chuck's arm tightened around the redhead's neck. "But she goes with us, just to make sure you don't get busy with other things and forget again."

Larry nodded. "Sure, go ahead and take her."

Kelly's eyes widened with terror, and Toby figured she'd be scream-ing curses at Larry if Chuck wasn't choking her. Chuck began to back away. Kelly started fighting and kicking. Chuck pulled the gun away from her head.

Toby expected Dana to shoot him when he did that. She could make a shot like that; Toby knew she could. But she didn't. She just stood motionless, her gun still leveled at Chuck's men. Larry didn't move, either, as Chuck slammed the gun against Kelly's head and stunned her so that she stopped struggling. He dragged her past the stairs and down a hall that led to the rear of the apartment. His men backed away, too. Gradually, they disappeared in the shadows at the end of the hall. A mo-ment later, Toby heard a door slam.

Larry heaved a sigh. "Sorry about that. I guess I'm not a very good host, am I?" He lowered his gun. "Now, what were we talking about before all that?"

4.

"You're going to just let them have her?" Toby said.

"She's a coked-up whore. She'll be dead in a few years anyway unless she cleans up her act, and that's not going to happen." Larry shook his head. "Besides, they'll just take her somewhere and fuck her for a couple of days. They won't kill her unless Chuck doesn't get his money."

Dana had lowered the automatic, too, but it was still in her hand. "Do you have the money to pay him?"

"Hey, we were talking about your problems, not mine," Larry said with a grin. "Let's get back to that, okay?"

"Not okay. Do you have the money to pay him?"

"Well ..." Larry scratched under his left ear and then shook his head. "No, not really."

Dana waved at the expensively-furnished apartment with her free hand and said, "All this, and you don't have the money?"

Toby heard a little ragged edge in her voice, but only he knew why it was there.

"Credit, darlin'. A guy's got to keep up appearances, you know. You live rich, people assume you *are* rich."

"You can't even come up with a hundred and fifty grand?"

Larry looked embarrassed now. "No, I don't suppose I can."

"The Lexus outside, that giant fucking TV ..."

"Like I said, credit." Larry was starting to get annoyed now. "I can't even sell the stuff. It's not really mine."

Toby saw Dana's breasts rising and falling as she breathed harder. He knew what she was thinking. Either she had been wrong about Larry stealing the money after the San Antonio bank job ... or he had managed to go through the whole four hundred thousand dollars in two years or less. Toby had an awful hunch it was the latter. Larry had expensive tastes. The proof of that was all around them. And beautiful redheaded teenagers with cocaine habits didn't come cheap, either.

"Why are you worried about this, Dana?" Larry said. "I'll be all right, you know that. I always find a way to land on my feet, don't I? And you've got problems of your own."

Dana took a deep breath and nodded. "You're right. I just ... Well, call me sentimental, but we've been together on enough jobs that I'd hate to see you wind up in the bottom of a gravel pit."

"Huh. You and me both." Larry put his gun away. "I need another drink." He started toward the bar but paused long enough to say to Toby, "You can put your gun up now, Junior. The bad mans have all gone away."

Larry turned his back, and Toby wondered just how much the blood and brains would splatter if he lifted the revolver and emptied it into the back of the bastard's head. Dana caught his eye, gave a slight shake of her head. Toby sighed and put the gun back in his pocket.

Larry tossed back a shot of whiskey, poured another, drank it, too. He wiped the back of his hand across his mouth. His face was flushed, whether from the liquor or emotion, Toby didn't know.

"I'll make some calls, see if I can't get hold of Gary or Walt."

"I appreciate that," Dana said, keeping up the act. Toby wasn't sure why she bothered, now that they knew Larry didn't have the money she needed to keep her from having to spend the rest of her life on the run.

"You know, something occurs to me," Larry said. "You came to me for help, Dana, and I'm glad to do what I can for you, but maybe you can help me, too."

She laughed. "I don't have a hundred and fifty thousand dollars. If I did ..." She shrugged. "Maybe I'd give you a hand. You'd owe me a big favor then."

"Hear me out. There's a favor you can do for me." He glanced at Toby. "You and the kid, if he's any good."

"I'll vouch for him."

Even under the circumstances, that simple statement made Toby feel good.

Larry nodded. "That's good enough for me."

"What did you have in mind?"

Larry poured another drink but just sipped from the glass this time. He licked his lips and said, "One last job. You and me, working together again, Dana, just like old times."

Dana hesitated. "You have something specific in mind?"

"Oh, yeah."

"Something big enough to get you out of the hole with Chuck?"

"More than big enough. I'm talking about at least half a million, probably more. We can even split the take three ways, if Toby's as good as you say he is."

Dana looked at Toby, and he guessed she was thinking that if Larry was right about the money, a third wasn't enough to make her problem go away. Even two-thirds wouldn't be.

But the whole amount would do the job, and that was what they could have if Larry was dead.

"Keep talking," Dana said.

Seven

1.

"It's an armored truck job," Larry said as they all sat down at a long, gleaming table in the dining room. "The truck makes the pickup from some of those big warehouse shopping clubs. Lots of cash."

"Where do we take it?"

"On the freeway when it's heading back to the bank, after the last pickup."

"On the freeway?" Toby said. "Won't there be a lot of people around?"

"I'm sure Larry has that covered," Dana said.

Larry grinned. "Sure I do. You know me, Dana, always trying to come up with something new. I've got my hands on a wrecker, one of those big jobs that can haul a semi truck."

"You're going to steal the whole armored truck?" Toby said.

"That's right, Junior."

Dana said, "You know, I don't think Toby cares for being called Junior."

"Oh, no offense meant," Larry said with a wave of his hand.

"Yeah, whatever," Toby said, not bothering to try to sound gracious about it.

"How do we get the truck stopped?" Dana asked.

"That'll be your job," Larry told her. "I was taking my time setting this up, but I thought all along I was going to need somebody like you and at least one man. You and the kid are perfect." He looked over at Toby. "Is 'kid' okay, or does that bother you, too?"

"Kid's fine. My name is Toby, though."

"Okay, okay." Larry swung his attention back to Dana. "The truck parks right out in front of the store while it's making the pickup. You'll plant a gadget I've whipped up under the front fender as you walk by. It's a little bomb, throws out enough shrapnel to shred a tire but mostly spews out a lot of smoke. When it goes off the guys on the truck will think they've had a blowout and that something else is wrong, maybe a fire in the engine. They won't have any choice but to stop on the side of the road. Then Toby and I pull up in the wrecker and offer to give them a hand."

"Won't they refuse and want to call their company? I would think that would be the normal procedure."

"Sure, but that's when the kid and I take them out."

"You mean kill them?" Toby said.

"You got a problem with that?"

Toby thought about it for a second. Dana needed that money if she was ever going to have any sort of a normal life. And maybe, just maybe, he could share part of that life with her.

"No, no problem," he said.

"Toby, are you sure?" Dana asked.

Larry shot a sharp look at her. "I thought you said you vouched for him."

"I do, but—"

Toby lifted a hand. "No, it's fine, Dana. Don't worry about me. I'll do whatever I need to do."

"You better be right, Toby," Larry said. "I'll be counting on you. You freeze at the wrong time and we could both wind up dead."

"You can count on me," Toby said.

Larry looked at him for a long moment and then nodded. "All right. I hope you're telling me the truth. I got no choice but to believe you."

That was just it. None of them had a choice, all the way around.

"There'll be at least one guard in the back of the truck," Dana said.

"Yeah, but he won't have time to do anything before we hook on to the truck with the wrecker and haul it out of there."

"He can call in the alarm and have every cop in the city looking for a wrecker hauling an armored car."

"Yeah, but we'll be off the road and inside a garage I've got lined up before anybody has a chance to spot us. I tell you, Dana, I've been working on this plan for a month. Nothing is going to go wrong."

Yeah, it might work, but even Toby, as inexperienced as he was, could see things that could go wrong. They would have to have luck on their side as well as Larry's planning. But that was the way he operated, Toby recalled Dana saying, and the fact that he was still alive and not in prison meant that his plans had been successful so far.

But one way or another, Larry Dunaway's luck was going to run out before too much longer.

2.

They spent another hour going over the details of the plan. Dana and

Larry seemed to have forgotten completely about Kelly. Since they weren't concerned about her, Toby tried not to be, either.

But he couldn't quite forget the look of sheer terror he had seen in her eyes. She'd been a little stoned, but not enough so that she didn't know what was going on. She had been aware of the ordeal facing her and of the fact that her life was in danger. Toby hadn't liked her, not even a little. Sure, she was sexy, but she was also stupid and unpleasant. No matter what happened to her, he wouldn't lose a lot of sleep over it. She sure had looked scared, though.

The fact that Larry was counting on him to help murder the armored car guards didn't bother him much. The guards would be well-armed. Even though Larry planned to take them by surprise, they'd have a chance. Maybe not much of one, but still, Toby and Larry would be risking their lives, too. That was just part of it, no way to avoid it.

"When?" Dana finally asked.

"Day after tomorrow," Larry said. "That gives me time to meet Chuck's deadline."

She nodded. "If we come through this alive, it'll be a good haul."

"Damn right it will."

Dana stood up. "Come on, Toby."

"Wait a minute," Larry said. "How can I get in touch with you?"

"You can't. I'll call you tomorrow. Give me your number."

Larry did so, grudgingly. "You still act a little like you don't trust me," he said. "We got to trust each other if we're going to pull this off."

"I trust you. It's just that being careful is a hard habit to break."

"Sure, I guess. You still want me to get in touch with Walt and Gary?"

Dana thought about it, or at least seemed to think about it. "Hold off on that," she said. "Let's get this job out of the way first, and then I'll try to settle things with them."

"All right. You're the boss, at least on that part of it."

They left shortly after that. It seemed almost impossible to Toby that only a few hours had passed since he and Dana first went to Deep Ellum looking for Larry. A lot had happened since then.

"I hope the boys behaved themselves," he said as they headed back to the motel with Dana at the wheel of the pickup.

"I do, too."

Everything was quiet when they arrived. No sounds came from inside the room. But as the key rattled in the door, Max and Clifford started barking loudly. He and Dana got inside as quickly as they could and hushed the dogs, who were overjoyed to see them.

Toby hooked the leashes to their halters and took them out for a walk. When he got back, Dana sat on the bed, nude. Toby let his eyes play over her, from the still-firm breasts to the triangle of dark blond hair over her pussy.

"Put the dogs in the bathroom," she said.

"Yes, ma'am."

"Don't call me ma'am."

Toby grinned and shut the dogs in the bathroom. They whined a little but didn't bark.

She practically tore his clothes off him. He didn't know if it was the danger they had faced during the stand-off with Chuck and his men, or the anticipation of the armored car job, or just pure arousal. Whatever the motivation, she got him naked and flat on his back on the bed in no time flat. She sucked on his penis for a while before straddling him and taking him inside her. When Toby finally came in her, she let out a little cry and then collapsed on top of him, huddling there and shivering slightly.

Later she rolled off of him and turned off the lamp beside the bed. The room was dark except for the strip of light that escaped under the bathroom door. The dogs had settled down and were probably asleep on the bath mat. Toby was drowsy, too, but couldn't seem to doze off.

"Are you asleep?" Dana said quietly.

"No."

"I thought that would help me unwind, but …"

"So that's all I am to you, a tranquilizer?"

She laughed, rolled onto her side, snuggled against him. After a moment she asked, "What do you think about Larry's plan?"

"You're the expert. You tell me."

"I never held up an armored truck before."

"Still, you know a lot more about this stuff than I do. Will it work?" She thought it over. "Probably."

"That's the best you can do?"

"No crime is foolproof. No matter how careful you are, things can happen that you didn't plan for. The big problem with Larry's plans is that he always expects things to break his way. That said, they usually do."

As she spoke, she trailed her fingers over his belly and into the hair at his groin. He began to get hard again.

He took hold of her wrist and said, "Not now. I want to know if you think we're going to get ourselves killed by going along with him."

"If I thought that I wouldn't have ever let him get the idea we might help him. This is our chance to get what we need." She moved away from him and sat up in bed. "That asshole! How could he go through that much money in such a short time? How did he manage to piss it all away?"

"High living? Expensive whores? Drugs? Gambling?"

Dana gave a humorless laugh. "E ... all of the above, more than likely."

"You're still sure he was the one behind the double-cross? That business about blaming Joyce or one of the others, that was just for Larry's benefit, right?"

"On her best day, Joyce was never smart enough to plan something like that. Gary or Walt might have, but they didn't. I know that."

"Like I said, you're the expert. I trust your judgment." He rubbed her back, sliding the flat of his hand over her smooth skin, feeling here and there a little mole that marred what was otherwise perfection, but in an intriguing way. "So we help Larry with this job, then double-cross him and take all the money. Right?"

"Right."

"We'll have to kill him."

"Yes."

"After that, what? Do you know how to get in touch with those other guys?"

"I can put out the word that I want to talk to them. They'll get the message."

"Then you give them the money and they don't bother you anymore."

"That's the plan," Dana said.

"But if they still think you double-crossed them, aren't they liable to want to get even with you for that?"

"It would be nice if I could get Larry to admit he was behind it, maybe even get that on tape so they could hear it. But the money is the most important thing. If they're satisfied with that, maybe they won't waste any more time and energy trying to kill me. I have to believe there's a way out. Otherwise, I might as well give up now."

Toby knew what it felt like to have to hang on to some hope, even a faint one.

"How would you ever get Larry to admit anything?"

Dana turned her head and looked down at him. In the dim light that came under the bathroom door, Toby couldn't see her face. But he could hear what was in her voice as she said, "Knowing Larry, that garage where we take the truck will be a nice, quiet place. The sort of place where nobody will hear, no matter what goes on there."

All Toby could say to that was, "Oh."

3.

He finally drifted off to sleep and didn't wake up until the next morning when Max and Clifford started whining at the door. Toby pulled his clothes on and took the dogs out. Dana was still in bed when he got back. He sat beside her and rubbed her back through the sheet.

"Oh, that feels good," she said.

"I can make you feel even better."

"Promises, promises ..."

Toby grinned and tugged the sheet down.

Later, as they lay together, wrapped up in each other's arms and legs, he wondered if it would always be like this. The hunger, the need for each other, couldn't stay this strong forever, could it? He didn't know, but it didn't seem possible. Surely it had to fade sooner or later.

Not that he would ever find out. Even if everything went perfectly and he and Dana took off for California or some other place with whatever money was left after paying off Walt and Gary, they wouldn't stay together forever. Nothing lasted forever, as he well knew.

But that was far enough down the road that he didn't have to think about it now.

They spent most of the day in the motel room, watching TV, napping, making love again. Toby brought in breakfast and lunch from one of the fast-food places. Late in the afternoon, they walked down to Wal-Mart, where Dana called Larry. Everything was going according to the plan. They would meet him at his place at eleven o'clock the next morning, and together they would drive the route they would take that afternoon.

For dinner that night they splurged and went to the Olive Garden and even had a bottle of wine with their food. Toby had a pleasant feeling about him when they got back to the motel. Not drunk, just ... pleasant.

Then Dana said, "We've got to talk about this before it's too late to call the whole thing off."

"Talk about what?"

"The fact that Larry's expecting you to help him kill those guards."

Toby was sitting at the foot of the bed with the dogs nuzzling against his legs. He looked down at them and said, "I don't want to talk about that."

"We have to."

"Why?"

"Because if you freeze, there's a good chance you'll wind up dead. Maybe Larry will, too. I don't care so much about what happens to Larry, except how it affects the money, but I don't want anything to happen to you, Toby."

He scratched Clifford's ears. "Don't tell me you've developed an undying love for me and couldn't live without me."

She leaned a hip against the dresser and folded her arms. "Don't be a jackass. You know I like you, but nobody ever said anything about love. Don't play innocent, either. I know why you came to the farm in the first place, remember?"

He looked up at her. "Are you sure about that?"

"You still thought I was really your mother when you fucked me the first time."

"How do you know? Maybe I'd already figured out that you weren't."

Dana shook her head. "You're not that good an actor."

"Yeah, well, maybe I knew it subconsciously. You don't really know what I would have done or why I came there."

"You came there because inside you're still the same scared, hurt little boy who didn't know why he'd been abandoned."

Toby came to his feet. "I'm not scared!"

"The hell you're not. We're all scared. Everybody. Because there's a big empty space out there at the end of everything, and sooner or later, you've got to step into it alone. We've all been abandoned, Toby. It's called being born."

He stared at her for a moment before looking away. "This doesn't have anything to do with what's going to happen tomorrow."

"Maybe, maybe not. Can you send somebody else out into that emptiness in order to postpone your own trip?"

"Sure I can."

"I hope you're right." She reached up and touched his face, resting her fingertips lightly on his cheek. "I'd hate to lose you right now, Toby."

"But you'd go right on if you did," he said.

"What other choice would I have? But I'd miss you, that's for sure."

Toby pulled her into his arms. "Nothing's going to happen to me," he said, his voice husky. "I'll do whatever I have to do."

"You know," she said, "I'm starting to believe you."

4.

They didn't make love that night, but they did the next morning. Toby woke up in the dawn with Dana snuggled against his back, her arm reaching over his hip so that she could stroke his erection. He rolled over to face her and they merged with a swift, hard urgency.

Nothing like the idea that you might be dead before the day was over to put a nice edge on a fuck.

Though it was a little hard to concentrate, they watched the morning news shows. It had been long enough now so that nothing was said about the murders on the farm and the disappearance of Grace Halligan. Whatever romance the story had had was gone now, dissipated by the lack of an arrest or any other new developments. When a year had gone by and the case was still unsolved, the anniversary might rate a brief mention in the newspaper. TV would ignore it. After that, it would have to be a damned slow news day before the case was ever dredged up again.

Toby got their breakfast and brought it back, then walked the dogs. When he returned to the room, Dana was stripping and cleaning all the guns. She had spread newspapers on the bed and had the greasy parts scattered out on them. Toby watched with admiration the way her hands worked with such smooth efficiency. She was good at what she did, no doubt about that.

"How in the world did you ever wind up being a bank robber?"

She glanced up at him. "You mean, what's a nice girl like you doing in a joint like this?"

"Yeah, something like that."

She shook her head. "You don't want my life story."

"How about part of it, then? I mean, my God, you look like a housewife. A hot, sexy housewife, mind you, but still a housewife."

She worked the action on the little automatic. "That's what I was, once. I don't know about the hot and sexy part, but I was married."

"Now, see, I didn't know that about you."

"It didn't last long. He was killed in a car wreck less than a year after the wedding."

"I'm sorry."

"It was a long time ago," she said with a shake of her head. "Twenty years."

"You didn't have any kids?"

"I was pregnant when Robbie was killed. I miscarried less than a week later."

Toby let out a low whistle. "That must have been rough."

"It was no picnic." She snapped a full clip up into the automatic's grip.

"What did you do then? Go back to your folks?"

"Are you kidding? I got married to get away from my parents. I was damned if I was going to come slinking back to them, begging for help."

"So what did you do?"

"I had a couple of years of college. I went to work in a lawyer's office, receptionist, mostly. One of his clients was a guy who owned a string of strip clubs in Fort Worth and Dallas. He offered me a job moonlighting as a dancer for him."

"You were a stripper?" Toby asked with a grin.

"Yeah. When I saw how much money I could make at that, I gave up the job in the law office."

"Well, you've got the body for it, that's all I can say."

Dana made a face. "Not anymore. Gravity takes its toll."

"Not on you. Not much, not yet."

"Thanks."

"How do you go from stripping to robbing banks?"

She started reassembling one of the revolvers. "You know the kind of guys who hang around strip clubs."

"Horny college boys?"

"Well, mostly," Dana said, smiling. "But there's a strong criminal element, too. Drugs and prostitution, you know. I stayed clear of both, didn't do any junk, didn't turn tricks. I saw how the girls who did aged so fast that they couldn't stay in the business more than a few years. I didn't mind the work and I liked the money, so I decided to keep myself in the best shape possible so I could hang around for longer. Even so, I met guys who were into all sorts of things."

"Like robbing banks."

She nodded. "Like robbing banks. Don't ask me how it got started. One of the guys asked me to come along on a job, I think. It's been so long … It was a joke, or a dare, like that. But I went along and drove, and I was good at it." She closed the revolver's cylinder. "Mighty oaks from little acorns grow."

"Yeah, I guess. So that's how you became a criminal."

"As much of the whole sordid story as I care to remember."

"So you've been robbing banks for, what, ten years?"

"Or twelve, somewhere along in there. But none the last two years, of course."

"Because you were hiding out on my mother's farm."

"Only part of that time, but hiding out, yeah."

"What are you going to do when all this is over?"

She looked at him and shook her head. "I don't know. I haven't thought that far ahead. Go out to the West Coast, try to disappear in the smog and the crowds. Get a job if I have to."

"There are banks in California."

"No," Dana said. "That's over. Once this job with Larry is finished, and when things are settled with Gary and Walt, I'm done with all that."

"That's good," Toby said, but he was thinking, sure, you are. She might want to live a normal life, but sooner or later the temptation would get too strong to resist.

Toby knew all about temptation, and how hard it was to resist.

5.

They checked out of the motel at ten-thirty. One way or the other, they wouldn't be coming back here. Dana drove the pickup across North Dallas, past Love Field, toward Larry's apartment. Traffic was heavy despite the mid-morning hour—traffic was always heavy in Dallas, Toby had decided—and it was just a few minutes before eleven when they got there.

Larry met them at the door and frowned. "Is that *barking* I hear?"

"We have dogs," Dana said.

"Okay. As long as they don't interfere with the job, it doesn't matter to me."

"They won't interfere." Dana would be leaving the pickup in the shopping club's parking lot while she planted the device on the armored truck. Max and Clifford could stay inside with the windows cracked. It would get hot inside the pickup pretty quickly, but Dana wouldn't be inside the store more than five minutes or so.

"Here's your membership card," Larry said, handing her a plastic oblong the size and shape of a credit card. "Can't get in the door without it."

Dana slipped it in her purse.

"Ready to go take a look? We can take the Lexus."

"Sure, but we have to do something with the dogs."

"Put 'em in my laundry room. They won't crap on the floor, will they?"

"No guarantees, but they're pretty well-behaved."

Toby rode in the back seat of the Lexus, Dana in the passenger seat up front. Larry was a fast but not reckless driver. "I've got it timed," he said. "The truck always gets there between two-thirty and two-forty. It's a busy time of day, lots of people coming and going. Nobody's going to pay any attention to you."

"They park right in front to pick up the money?" Toby said. "Seems to me like they'd at least go in the back."

"The office is upstairs in the front. It's handier to take the money out that way. Besides, it's all routine. They've gotten sloppy because nothing has ever happened and they don't think it ever will. Think about it. How many armored trucks have you seen parked in front of businesses? Nobody pays attention to them anymore."

Toby decided Larry was right. Over the years, he had probably walked past dozens of armored trucks making pickups or deliveries at various businesses. And he had never given them a second thought, either.

Of course, that had been before he was a professional criminal.

The shopping club was near the intersection of two freeways. Larry drove through the parking lot and pointed out the entrance and exit doors, which were some fifty feet apart. "That's where the truck will be parked, between those doors." A steady stream of people moved into and out of the huge, boxy building. "From here the truck pulls out of the parking lot onto the service road and then onto the freeway and heads west toward the bank. Toby and I will be in the wrecker, parked over there at that car dealership that's out of business." He pointed it out. "We'll see the truck go past and will fall in behind it, giving it a little lead."

"You went over all this yesterday," Toby said.

"It's different when you're actually on the ground. Pay attention, kid."

"I'm paying attention. Don't worry about that. I guess you'll have a detonator to set off the explosive?"

"That's right. Range of a mile, line of sight, but I won't let the truck get that far ahead of us. More like half a mile or so."

"So you blow the little bomb, the truck pulls over, and you pull up in front with the wrecker."

Larry nodded. "Then we get rid of the guards, hook on to the truck, and get the hell out of there." He was on the freeway by now and waved at the shoulder. "Somewhere along in here, I hope. From here it takes a minute to get to where another highway loops off to the north. We take it, and another minute or two later we're pulling off into an industrial district. That's where the garage is. If everything goes according to plan, it'll be less than five minutes after we start off towing the truck until we're inside the garage and out of sight."

He showed them the exits and the garage, then turned the Lexus back toward his apartment.

"We do the split in the garage," Dana said.

Larry frowned. "I figured we'd just take the money back to my place and divvy it up there. We all have to go back there anyway if I'm going to get in touch with Gary and Walt."

"No, I'd rather do it like I said. You can go back to your apartment by yourself. I'll call you later."

Larry shrugged. "Suit yourself. It doesn't really matter to me."

"Well, that's the way I want it."

Of course, none of them would be going back to Larry's apartment, because the odds were that Larry would be dead by then, and he and Dana would have all the money.

"Everything look all right to you?" Larry asked.

Dana nodded. "Yes. Let's do this."

Eight

1.

None of them felt like eating lunch. Dana and Larry were too cool to admit they were nervous, but Toby was willing to bet that was why they weren't hungry. As for himself, he was jumpy, and there was no point in denying it, especially to himself.

Yet deep down, he knew he would do okay. He wasn't going to panic or freeze or do any of the things Dana was worried he might do. Once everything got started, he would be all right.

They went back to Larry's place, where Toby walked the two dogs in the tiny back yard. Then he put them in the pickup.

"Wear this," Larry said to him when he came back inside. He held out some coveralls toward Toby.

He took them and held them up. They were gray, short-sleeved, and had the name "Vince" stitched into them with red thread.

"I ask you, do I look like a Vince?"

Larry grunted. "You look enough like one to me. Put 'em on. Dana can take your regular clothes in the pickup."

"Sure." Toby carried the coveralls into the bathroom to change.

When he came out, Larry asked him, "Do you have a gun?"

Toby held up the bundle of clothes in his arms. "In my pants pocket."

"Get it. Unless you'd rather use one of mine."

"No, this one will be okay." Toby dug the gun out of the clothes. He wished he had had a chance to practice with it. What could go wrong, though? All you had to do was make sure it was loaded, then point it and pull the trigger.

The side pocket in the coveralls was plenty big for the revolver. Toby drew it from there a few times just to get the feel of it. Dana watched him with a faint smile on her face. Larry had gone off to change into his own set of coveralls.

"That's quite a fast draw you've got," she said.

"Fast enough, I hope."

"You'll have the element of surprise on your side. That's enough to give you a big advantage."

"How surprised are they really going to be? They're guards, after all. They have to be trained to expect trouble."

"They're former cops or ex-military, most of them. Tough and in good shape, probably, but not at their peak anymore. They're just employees, drawing a wage. They do their jobs, go home, and forget about it. You can take them."

Toby drew in a deep breath. "I know. I won't let you down." He came closer to Dana and lowered his voice. "What about in the garage ...?"

"Just follow my lead," she said. "You'll be able to tell what to do. Just remember ... if you have to move, move quick, for God's sake."

He nodded.

Larry came out, wearing coveralls with the name "Ted" on them. "Ready to go?"

"Yeah, Ted," Toby said. "Ted and Vince, wrecker drivers, that's us."

Larry gave Dana a key. "After you leave the store, head for the garage and park around behind it. There's a back door. This key will let you in there. You can wait for us there. It shouldn't be long before we show up."

"Okay." She slipped the key in her pocket.

"And here's the other little gizmo."

It was flat and a little smaller than a 3.5 inch computer disk. The case was dull-colored metal.

"It's magnetized," Larry said. "All you've got to do is slip it inside the wheel well of the truck. They'll never see it."

Dana turned it over in her hands. "It can't go off on its own, can it?"

"It's perfectly harmless until it receives the signal from the detonator."

She nodded but looked a little uneasy as she put it in the same pocket where she had stowed the key. She turned to Toby. "Be careful."

He took her in his arms, not caring that Larry was standing right there a few feet away. "You, too." He kissed her.

After a moment, Larry said, "This is touching as hell, but we'd better get a move-on. It'd really suck if we were too late to get that truck today."

"Yeah, because Chuck plans on killing you tonight," Toby said as he stepped away from Dana.

Larry stared at him with dead eyes. "You got a big mouth, kid. If you weren't with Dana, I'd shut it for you."

Dana moved between them and said, "Listen, you two have to be able to work together. Quit sniping at each other."

"Yeah, you're right," Toby said. "I'm sorry, Larry. I do have a big mouth."

Larry just grunted and then said, "Let's go."

2.

Dana drove off in the pickup. Larry and Toby took the Lexus and headed back across town toward the garage. That was where the wrecker was stashed, Larry explained.

He seemed to have gotten over being irritated. He asked as he drove, "How did you and Dana wind up together, anyway?"

Toby couldn't tell if he was really interested or was just making small talk to help ward off the nerves. "We just ran into each other and hit it off, that's all."

"Where?"

"I don't remember." They had agreed not to talk about anything that had happened on the farm. All that would be just between them, forever.

Larry laughed. "Hell, I'm your partner now, kid. You don't have to be close-mouthed with me."

"Dana and I just prefer to keep certain things private."

"Yeah, I'll bet you do. I never got into her pants myself, but you can tell by looking at her she's one hell of a lay."

Toby looked out the passenger side window. He didn't like hearing Larry talk about Dana like that, but he wasn't going to let himself get mad. He didn't know why Larry was picking at him. Under the circumstances, it seemed like it would have been better to keep things calm, with no hard feelings on either side.

Some guys just couldn't let things go, though, and it looked like Larry was one of them.

"She was a wild one, though, back in the day. I heard a lot of stories about her. Once she was in on a job with three guys, and they sealed the deal by taking turns fucking her, one right after the other. I ain't much on snowballin', you know, but for a chance to get in that pussy, I'd have done it."

Toby clenched his right hand into a fist and beat a gentle tattoo on his thigh.

"One night down in San Antone, before that job came off, I tried to get her into bed with Joyce and me, get some of that good old girl-girl action going, you know. Joyce liked to eat a little pussy now and then, when the mood was right. But Dana wasn't having any. I think the world and all of her, you know, but she can be a snooty bitch when she wants to. Thought she was too good to have a little fucky-sucky with us." Larry laughed. "Damned if she probably wasn't right. I got to admit, she is a mite higher class than me. Don't you think, Toby?"

He forced himself to say, "I never thought about it."

"Aw, hell, might as well admit it. You think ol' Larry's a sleazebag, don't you?"

"I never thought about that, either."

"Sure you did. And it's not like I set out to be such a crude son of a bitch. Just sort of happened that way. Everybody's an asshole to somebody. Some of us just have a broader spectrum through which to spread our offensiveness."

Toby couldn't help it. He laughed. Larry grinned over at him.

"There you go. You ready, kid?"

Toby saw that they were at the garage.

"I'm ready," he said.

3.

The garage door had an automatic opener on it. Larry pressed a button on a hand-held control in the Lexus, and the thick, sheet-metal door began to roll up on its tracks. Larry drove inside and parked next to a large tow truck. It was almost the size of a diesel cab without the trailer. The door rattled back down, leaving the interior of the garage in shadow. One small, barred window high in the rear wall let in a little light.

"You know how to drive one of these suckers?" Larry asked as they got out of the Lexus.

"I'm afraid not."

"That's all right, I do. You got shotgun."

"And I didn't even have to call it."

"That's right, there's just you and me, pard."

They climbed into the wrecker, using the steps on the sides to do so. The cab reeked of cigarette smoke. Toby wrinkled his nose.

"Don't like the smell?" Larry said. "It was that way when I got it. Guy who had it before must've smoked like a chimney. I don't use the stuff myself, 'cept for a little weed now and then. We'll roll down the windows, and it won't be so bad once we get going."

"There's no air conditioner?"

"Naw, this baby's got that good old four-sixty air conditioning, only it'd be two-sixty because there's only two windows."

The engine started with a rumbling roar when Larry turned the key. The noise and the vibration reminded Toby of the tractor back on the farm in West Texas. He had liked that, but he didn't care much for this. The noise was uncomfortably loud inside the thick concrete walls of the garage.

Larry used the opener to raise the door. He and Toby rolled the windows down as he drove out. Then he paused and handed the remote to Toby. "Stick your arm out the window and close the door, okay?"

Toby took the little gadget, pointed it back at the garage, and pressed the button. The door descended with a rattle.

"Good thing I handed you the right remote," Larry said. "The wrong one might've set off that bomb in Dana's pocket."

"Don't even joke about it," Toby said.

"Well, see, that's where you don't understand me, kid. I can joke about anything. Anything and everything. You know why that is?"

"Because you don't take anything seriously?" Toby said as Larry turned the wrecker and sent it rolling along the street through the industrial district.

"Nope. It's because I take *everything* seriously. You can't really make fun of something if you don't care about it."

Toby shrugged and didn't say anything. He could see Larry's point, but they weren't here to debate such things.

"No air conditioning, but the radio works," Larry said. "You mind a little music?"

"Go ahead."

Larry punched the power button. The throbbing sounds of dance music filled the cab. Toby didn't like it much, and he was surprised Larry did. Larry was too old for techno. But then, he was too old to have been hanging around that club where they'd found him in Deep Ellum, too. Maybe he was one of those guys who never wanted to admit, even to himself, how old he really was.

Larry beat time on the steering wheel. They were on their way to commit murder and steal half a million dollars, and Larry was acting like he was heading out to a party. Maybe that's all it was to him.

Too late to worry about such things. There was the shopping club with its crowded parking lot. Toby leaned forward without thinking about it as his eyes searched the rows of cars for Dana's pickup.

Grace Halligan's pickup, actually. *Hope you're proud of your little boy, Mom, wherever you are.*

Larry drove past the shopping club. "You see her?"

"No, I … Wait a minute! There she is! She's heading inside."

Larry slowed the wrecker. "What about the armored truck?" he asked, his voice crackling with tension. "Is the truck there?"

"Right in front of the store. Right where it's supposed to be."

Larry killed the radio and pounded the steering wheel with the flat of his hand. "Yes! It's all going to work."

He drove along the service road for a couple of hundred yards before reaching the closed-down car dealership. He pulled into the driveway, past the now-empty lot, and circled beside the service bays so that the wrecker was pointed back out. From here they could see the ramp the armored truck would take when it entered the freeway. All they had to do was wait.

And hope that Dana was able to plant the bomb without being spotted.

4.

The waiting was harder than Toby thought it would be. He slipped the revolver from the pocket of his coveralls and checked it over, even though he knew that wasn't necessary. Larry said, "Take it easy, kid. It won't be long now."

"How long is the truck usually there?"

"Thirty minutes, tops." Larry glanced at his wristwatch. "They'll be along here around three o'clock."

It was five minutes until three when Larry's cell phone rang. He took it out of his pocket, flipped it open, and said, "Yeah?" A grin spread across his face. "All right." He closed the phone and put it away.

"Dana?" Toby said.

"Yeah. They're on the way. Everything went fine. The gizmo's in the right front wheel well. It'll pull the truck toward the shoulder when it blows. Don't want it veering into traffic in the other lane and causing a wreck. That would ruin everything."

"What if the truck's in the inside lane?"

"It won't be. The driver's planning on exiting just a little ways up the road, remember? Besides, the gadget doesn't go off until I tell it to. I'll wait for the right moment."

Larry started the wrecker again. Toby stared through the bug-splattered windshield. He told himself that he felt calm, but his jaw was tight and from time to time he felt a little muscle in his face jump.

Half a million dollars, he told himself. And freedom for Dana.

Besides, Larry really *was* a sleazebag. He deserved to die.

"There it is," Larry said in a hushed voice as the armored truck rolled past on the service road, angling toward the freeway entrance. "Ready?"

"Ready," Toby said, a little surprised at how firm his voice sounded.

With a clash of gears, the wrecker started forward. Larry pulled out of the dealership parking lot and angled onto the freeway. Toby saw the armored truck ahead of them. It seemed to him that the truck was building up speed faster than the wrecker and was pulling away from them. "What if they get too far ahead of us for the detonator to work?" he asked.

"They won't." Larry took the detonator from the pocket of his coveralls. "Check for cops. We don't want one pulling over to see what's wrong."

Toby tried to look in all different directions at once. When he realized what he was doing, he took a breath and methodically checked all the mirrors and as far ahead on the opposite side of the freeway as he could see.

"Nothing."

"Good. Here we go, right ...*now.*"

Larry pointed the detonator and triggered it.

Toby saw the sudden puff of smoke. The truck swerved sharply onto the wide shoulder and weaved back and forth. Dust flew in the air as the right-side wheels left the pavement and hit dirt and gravel. A second later, the truck shuddered to a stop. White smoke continued to come from the right front wheel well, not a lot but enough to be a concern to the driver and the other guards.

Only a few cars were between the wrecker and the armored truck. Toby saw brake lights flare as the drivers caught sight of the disabled truck, but none of the vehicles stopped or even slowed down much. They zipped on past, their drivers intent on their own business, their own destinations.

Larry tromped harder on the wrecker's accelerator. The distance closed faster than Toby expected it to. Suddenly, they were there. Larry pulled onto the shoulder in front of the truck and then backed up a few yards, the wrecker's horn beeping automatically as he did so. He brought the wrecker to a stop but left the engine running. Then he looked over at Toby and nodded.

Toby put his hand on the revolver through the fabric of the coveralls and opened the passenger door. He dropped easily to the ground and started back toward the truck. The driver and the other guard up front had already piled out and were hovering around the shredded tire. One of the men had a small chemical fire extinguisher in his hand and bent over to squirt the foam into the wheel well.

Off to the side of the shoulder, a grassy embankment rose about twenty feet where the service road lifted to an overpass, cutting off the view in that direction. The truck itself shielded the freeway. Larry had picked a near-perfect spot.

"You guys need some help?" Larry said as he stepped between the back of the wrecker and the front of the armored truck.

The harried-looking guards barely glanced at him and Toby. "No, we'll call it in," one of them said. "The company will send somebody out."

Larry bent down beside the one with the fire extinguisher. "What the hell happened, a blowout?"

"Yeah—" the man began, but then Larry brought out his gun and shot him in the head, one quick bark of a shot that snapped the man's head to the side and sent him slumping against the truck's fender. Larry grabbed his arm to keep him from falling all the way to the ground. Passersby might be more likely to notice that.

At the same time, Toby pulled the revolver from his pocket, held it close to him, and shot the other guard. The bullet hit the man in the right side and drove him back a step, but he didn't fall. Although he gasped and turned pale, he was able to reach for the heavy gun holstered on his hip.

Before Toby could fire again, Larry turned slightly and snapped a shot that took the second guard in the forehead. A black hole appeared over his right eye. He slumped against the open door of the truck.

"Get him in the cab!" Larry said. Toby jammed the revolver back in his pocket and leaped forward to grab the second guard. He shoved the man through the door onto the floorboards. The dead guard flopped, half in, half out, like a fish in a boat. Toby caught hold of his legs, lifted them, and shoved. The guard slid across the floorboard.

Larry had the other man there by then, holding him up like he was sick or something, and they shoved him into the cab on top of the other man. Larry slammed the door. Less than thirty seconds had passed since the first shot.

As Larry hurried back to the front of the truck, Toby realized that he had neglected to tell him how the wrecker's lift mechanism operated. That didn't matter, though. Larry knew what he was doing, and with swift, concise directions, he told Toby how to help him hook up the truck for towing. When it was ready, he slapped Toby on the shoulder and said, "Go."

They hurried back to the cab of the wrecker. Larry engaged a lever, and with a loud whine, the hook and the bar under the front of the truck raised it into the air until the front wheels were well off the ground. Larry locked everything in place, put the wrecker in gear, and drove away, towing the armored truck behind them.

5.

"You fucking idiot! Head shots! Didn't you ever hear of bulletproof vests?"

"Nobody told me," Toby said. "I didn't even think about it."

"Fucking idiot!"

The wrecker's engine roared under the load of pulling the armored truck. Larry swung through a long, curving exit that led onto another freeway. This one would take them to the garage, less than a mile away.

Toby wondered what was going on in the back of the truck. Was the guard there frantically calling his superiors on a radio or cell phone? Had the alarm already gone out to the police?

Larry was overreacting. True, Toby had failed to kill the other guard with his first shot, but he would have fired again. Larry just hadn't given him the chance.

He hoped Larry wouldn't tell Dana about it. He didn't want her to be disappointed in him.

And maybe it was true that he did need a little more practice before he could consider himself a professional criminal. Still, as far as he could tell, everything was going all right so far.

Larry drew a deep breath. "When we get to the garage, you stand back and cover me. I'll handle the guy in the back."

"How do you know there's somebody back there?"

"There always is, on pickup runs like this. If there isn't for some reason, we'll just consider it a bonus. And on second thought, stay the hell out of the way. Dana will be there, and she's all the back-up I need."

Toby swallowed his anger. Larry thought he was a fuck-up, just because nobody had told him that the guards would be wearing bulletproof vests and he hadn't thought of it on his own. That wasn't fair. Larry couldn't hold it against him for not thinking of it when he himself hadn't thought to mention it.

And anyway, it didn't really matter what Larry thought. He wasn't going to be alive for that much longer.

Toby watched the truck in the big side mirror. It seemed to be riding just fine. Larry pulled off the freeway and took the side street that led toward the garage. A minute later, they were there.

Without waiting for Larry to tell him, Toby picked up the remote control and activated the garage door. It rose in its tracks. Larry pulled straight in. The garage was deep enough so that the door would close behind the armored truck. Toby pushed the button again, starting it down.

Overhead fluorescent lights flickered into life. Dana must have turned them on. As Larry turned off the wrecker's engine, Toby saw Dana run from the rear of the building toward them. The little automatic was in her hand.

Larry and Toby dropped from opposite sides of the cab. Toby hurried around the front of the wrecker while Larry trotted alongside the armored truck. The door in the back of the truck would be locked, and it would be a waste of time trying to convince the guard inside to open it. Larry went to a workbench, opened a metal box there, and took out a blob of something that Toby knew was plastic explosive. He fastened it on the truck's rear door.

Dana came up to Toby. "Are you all right?"

He jerked his head in a nod. "Everything went fine," he said. "All according to plan."

"It's always that way for Larry."

But not anymore.

Larry ducked around the rear corner of the truck, and a couple of seconds later the explosive went off with a muted blast. Anybody outside the garage could have heard that, but not many people were around here. The walls would muffle the sound so much that it would be difficult to tell where it came from.

Larry rushed to the mangled door, jerked it open even more, and emptied his gun into the compartment inside the truck. The guard must have been stunned by the explosion. He didn't get a shot off. As Toby and Dana came around the back of the truck, Toby glanced inside and saw the sprawled, bloody figure of the guard. Larry's shots had blown off a considerable portion of his head.

Toby's stomach lurched unexpectedly. He hadn't thought there would be quite so much blood. He swallowed as Larry grabbed the dead guard's feet and dragged him out of the truck, letting the corpse fall heavily to the cement floor where it would be out of the way. Then Larry climbed in and started handing out canvas satchels to Toby and Dana.

It took a while to unload half a million dollars. At least it seemed that way to Toby. "Put it in the Lexus," Larry said.

"I'm riding with you," Dana said. "Toby can bring the pickup."

Larry grinned. He would expect Dana to be suspicious at a time like this. "Sure, babe," he said.

Finally, all the money was loaded into the back seat of the Lexus. Toby wondered why Dana was waiting so long to kill Larry. Maybe she had wanted him to help with the money before she got rid of him.

He was happy, grinning and saying, "We did it, goddamn, we fucking did it. Half a million, minimum." He looked like a kid at a birthday party.

Toby reminded himself of how Larry had double-crossed Dana after the bank job in San Antonio, how his betrayal had marked her for death and sent her on the run for two years, never knowing when sudden violence was going to catch up to her, as it had on the farm. Whatever happened next, Larry had it coming.

Larry tossed Toby a rag. "Wipe down the cab of the wrecker."

"Sure." Toby wiped the handle on the passenger door, then used the rag to open it.

As the door opened, two shots blasted from the back of the wrecker. The glass in the window shattered and sprayed over Toby.

Nine

1.

Toby let out an involuntary yell and dropped to his knees. He twisted around, feeling pain as some of the shattered glass cut through his coveralls and into his right knee. He jerked the revolver from his pocket, brought it up ready to fire.

He saw Larry lurch away from the wrecker, stumbling a little as he ran. Beyond Larry, Dana stood with the automatic leveled, left hand bracing right wrist as she fired again. The bullet smacked into Larry and drove him off his feet. He slid across the dirty concrete floor, leaving dark smears in the coating of dust. The gun slipped from his fingers and clattered away from him. He tried to push himself up but couldn't do it. He sagged back with a sigh.

"Toby!" Dana said. "Are you all right?"

His knee hurt like blazes where the broken glass had cut it, but he told himself to ignore the pain. "Yeah."

"Get his gun."

Toby stood up and hurried toward Larry. Larry's eyes were open and he looked up at Toby with more hatred than seemed possible for one human being to muster. "You ... you bastards ..." he said.

As Toby scooped up the fallen gun, Dana said, "You were about to shoot me in the back, Larry. You were going to double-cross us just like you did to me in San Antonio, so don't come crying to me."

Larry twisted his head so that he could look at her. His gray coveralls were almost black in places now as blood soaked into them. "Stupid ... cunt. You never ... had a chance. Almost too easy ... setting you up."

Dana reached in her pocket with her left hand while the right kept the gun pointed at Larry. "You were behind the whole thing, weren't you, Larry?" she said, and Toby knew she had pressed the record button on the little recorder she must be carrying. "You double-crossed Walt and Gary and the rest of us and stole that four hundred grand."

"Stupid ... cunt," he said again.

"And then you ran through all the money, so you don't have it anymore."

"Go to hell!" Larry grated out the words, then arched his back and screamed in pain.

Toby stepped up to him and kicked him hard in the head. Larry's skull bounced off the cement floor, and he went limp and quiet.

"You shouldn't have done that," Dana said. "He hadn't admitted that he was responsible for that other double-cross."

"He wasn't going to," Toby said. "You heard him."

"It wasn't your call to make. It wasn't you he betrayed."

"Well, then, let's wait for him to wake up, and then we'll work on him some more. After some of the things he said, I wouldn't mind doing that."

Dana shook her head. She came closer to Larry, knelt beside him, felt for a pulse in his neck. "I doubt if he'll ever regain consciousness. He'll bleed to death in another five minutes. Time for us to get out of here." As she straightened, she looked at Toby's leg and said, "Did that wild shot he fired hit you?"

He glanced down, saw the bloodstain on the leg of the coveralls. "No, it broke the window, and some of that broken glass cut me when I ducked. What the hell happened, anyway?"

"He was about to shoot me in the back. I turned around and got a shot off first, and that hit him and threw off his aim."

Toby heaved a sigh. "What now?"

"We take the money and get out of here."

"What about him?" Toby waved a hand toward Larry's sprawled body.

"We don't have to worry about him anymore. Like I said, he won't last another five minutes." A wistful note entered her voice. "I just wish he was awake to suffer some more before he fades out." She opened the door of the Lexus. "You drive the pickup and follow me. We'll go back to Larry's place, pick up the dogs, and transfer the money there."

Toby nodded. "Okay."

She gave him the keys to the pickup. He went out the back door of the garage and found it parked in the alley behind the building. By the time he got in, started the engine, and drove around front, the big door was coming up. Dana gunned the Lexus out when the door was barely high enough for the car to clear. The door started to rumble back down behind her.

The neighborhood seemed quiet. The blast of the plastic explosive and the gunshots that had followed it had gone, if not unnoticed, then ignored. Within minutes, the Lexus and the pickup were both back on the freeway, following it as it looped around Dallas and led back toward the area where Larry had lived.

Now that it was over, Toby felt reaction setting in. He had to hold tightly to the steering wheel to keep his hands from trembling. His guts felt hollow. His knee throbbed where the glass had cut it. He kept his eyes on the Lexus, knowing that if Dana got away from him, he might never find his way back to Larry's.

But why would she want to get away from him? They were partners, right? She wouldn't turn on him, the way Larry had done once to her and had just tried to do again. They had planned to double-cross Larry and take the money, but he had saved them the trouble by trying to betray them first. He should have seen it coming. No doubt that was just what Dana had expected Larry to do all along.

Half a million dollars, quite possibly more, right up there in that Lexus. Say they got in touch with Gary and Walt and paid them off, gave them the whole four hundred thousand Larry had stolen. That would be enough to get them off Dana's back, and it would still leave a minimum of a hundred thousand for the two of them to go somewhere and start over. A hundred grand wasn't nearly what it used to be, but it would keep someone in pretty comfortable style for a year or so.

And a lot of other things could happen in a year's time. The future was out there just waiting for him to grab it.

2.

Max and Clifford were overjoyed to see them, as always. One of the dogs had left a pile of shit on the laundry room floor in Larry's apartment. Judging by the size of the pile, Max was responsible. Toby gave him an extra scratch behind the ears and said, "Good boy, good boy."

Dana took a quick look through the apartment, gun in hand. No one else was there. Chuck had given Larry forty-eight hours, and the time wouldn't be up until that evening. It didn't hurt to be careful, though. Chuck could have decided to get there early.

If he came on time, he would find nothing but an empty apartment. Larry was gone and wouldn't be coming back.

Toby wondered for a moment what would happen to Kelly. Chances were she would wind up dead and buried in a shallow grave somewhere out in the country. That was a damned shame, because she'd been pretty sexy. But it was Larry's fault for being such an asshole and making enemies of guys like Chuck, and Kelly's own fault for taking up with Larry in the first place.

He and Dana were looking out for themselves. They couldn't be expected to save the whole fucking world.

"Do we count the money here?" he asked.

Dana shook her head. "Just move it from the Lexus to the pickup and then let's get out of here. I've had enough of this place."

"Yeah, me, too."

Dana had pulled the Lexus all the way to the back, stopping in the little garage at the rear of the duplex. Toby had parked the pickup right behind her. Now, as Toby started through the door that led from the kitchen and laundry room area into the garage, he heard a car door slam somewhere nearby.

Dana heard it, too. She motioned for Toby to stop and come back. He eased the door closed.

"Chuck?" he asked in a whisper.

Dana shrugged and shook her head. She didn't know.

With a curt gesture she sent him to the front room of the apartment. Keeping low, he went to the window. It hurt his injured knee to crouch like that, but he did it anyway, wanting to stay out of sight. Curtains covered the window, but there was a slight gap between them. Toby edged up to it and risked a look. From there he could see the back end of a car parked in the driveway, but that was all.

The doorbell rang.

Dana shook her head. The front door was locked. They could hope that Larry's visitor would just go away when no one answered the summons.

The bell rang again. If whoever it was looked along the driveway to the rear of the place, they would see the pickup parked in front of the garage. Would that make them even more determined to get in?

One worry had been pretty well disposed of by the events of the past few seconds. The visitor wasn't Chuck. Chuck and his men would not have parked out front in plain sight, and they wouldn't ring the doorbell. They would have gotten in some other way if they intended to set a trap for Larry. This might be as innocent as somebody selling something.

Why the hell didn't they just go away? Surely by now they realized that nobody was home.

The doorbell rang for a third time. Somehow, it had the sound of finality about it, probably the way it was cut off so shortly. Toby's taut nerves eased slightly. Now, the visitor would go away.

A key scraped in the lock.

3.

In the arched doorway between the living room and the dining area, Dana made a chopping motion with her free hand. Toby interpreted that to mean for him to get out of sight. He went down on hands and knees and scrambled behind a long, heavy sofa while Dana ducked back around the corner with the automatic now held in both hands in front of her face. Toby pulled the revolver from the pocket of his coveralls as he lay on the thick carpet. His knee throbbed from the pressure he had put on it by crawling.

A couple of seconds dragged by in silence. Then the door opened, and Toby heard someone step into the room. The door closed. Keys jingled. A woman's voice called, "Larry? Larry, are you here?"

Toby didn't recognize the voice, and to the best of his memory he had never heard it before. Another of Larry's many girlfriends, more than likely. The woman moved deeper into the room. Toby hunkered against the back of the sofa as hard as he could.

"Larry?" she said again as she came into view. Now if she turned her head to the left, she could see Toby lying there, just as he could see her. She was slender and elegant in expensive boots, jeans, and a lacy white blouse. Around thirty, she was stunningly pretty, with thick brown hair that fell around her shoulders. Toby had never seen her before.

"Damn it, Larry, you're such a prick," the woman said, and Toby couldn't argue with that. She stepped toward the doorway. If she moved on into the dining area, Dana could knock her out with a swift blow from the automatic, and they could get out of here without the woman ever getting a good look at them.

Instead, the woman stopped short and jerked her head toward Toby, her eyes widening as she stared straight at him. Toby figured she was about to scream.

She didn't. Instead, she dropped the fashionable little purse she had been carrying, but not before she plucked a gun from it and leveled it at him. "Don't move!" she said.

Dana came around the corner behind the woman. "Drop it, Joyce!"

she said. "I'll kill you if you don't!" The automatic in Dana's hands was lined on the back of the woman's head.

Joyce … ? That was the name of—

"Dana, is that you?" Joyce said.

"Yes, it is, and you know I'll do what I say."

Joyce smiled. "Yes, but you can't kill me in time to stop me from putting a bullet in your friend over there. I assume that young man is your friend?"

"Cover her, Toby," Dana said.

"No!" Joyce said. "If he lifts his gun I fire, Dana. I might as well."

"You fucking bitch."

"At least I don't steal from my friends."

"Neither do I!"

"What about that four hundred thousand?"

"I never took that money! Larry did."

Joyce laughed. "He said you'd say that."

"What?"

"He called me yesterday, told me that you were back and spinning some wild story about how he was responsible for that double-cross in the Hill Country. He said you wanted to meet with me and Gary and Walt and beg for forgiveness. I told him that wouldn't be enough, especially for Gary and Walt. All they want is the money."

"So what are you doing here?"

Joyce still had her gaze riveted on Toby over the barrel of her gun. "I thought I'd hear you out," she said. "I always liked you, Dana. I thought maybe I could forgive you."

"There's nothing to forgive. I didn't do it."

Toby swallowed hard and said, "Ladies, could you possibly have this discussion without the pointing of guns? I'm getting a little tired of laying here, and my knee hurts like hell."

"Stay where you are," Joyce said. "Who is he, Dana? What are you really doing here?"

"Trying to set things right," Dana said.

"Where's Larry?"

"Gone."

Toby knew that was a mistake as soon as Dana said it. Something odd came into Joyce's eyes, and even though she had left Larry for the other two men, Toby suspected she still had feelings for him.

"You killed him." The words were a flat accusation, not a question.

"He didn't give me any choice," Dana said.

With a shrill cry, Joyce spun to the side, bringing her gun around. Dana fired, but the shot missed and the bullet smacked into the wall on the far side of the room. Joyce's toe caught the handle of the purse she had dropped and sent it flying through the air toward Dana's face. Dana flinched involuntarily before she could squeeze off another shot. Joyce's gun blasted and Dana cried out in pain.

"No!" Toby said as he came up off the floor, not thinking about what he was doing, just acting. He crashed into Joyce, but it was only a glancing blow as she tried to jerk herself out of his way. Toby tripped on something and went down, landing hard on the floor.

Another gunshot roared, and this time Joyce let out a gasp of pain. Toby looked up from the floor and saw blood on the left sleeve of her blouse, the red stark against the white fabric. She was half turned away from him. He kicked her in the back of the knee. She gasped again and went down, but she fired as she fell. Dana said, "Shit!"

A gun slid across the floor about ten feet from Toby. He recognized it as Dana's automatic. She had dropped it for some reason, probably because Joyce had wounded her again.

Dana could still move, though, and she wheeled toward Joyce with a roundhouse kick. The blow struck Joyce on the arm and sent that gun flying as well. Now both women were unarmed.

But far from helpless. Joyce's other hand shot up, grabbed Dana's leg, heaved hard. Dana went over backward. Joyce scrambled after her. A hand slashed toward Dana's face. She blocked the blow at the last second, struck back with one of her own, knocking Joyce to the side. Joyce recovered instantly and snapped a vicious kick to Dana's midsection as both women lay on the floor.

Toby tried to get up, but his left leg wouldn't work for some reason. He figured he must have hurt it when he tripped and fell. He started crawling toward the nearest gun, which happened to be Dana's automatic. As he dragged himself along he threw a glance over his shoulder and saw that Dana and Joyce had both regained their feet. Their arms and legs were blurs as they attacked each other. It was like something out of a martial arts movie. The Deadly Fists of the Bank Robbing Soccer Moms. He would have laughed if he hadn't been so scared and in so much pain.

He heard a crash behind him as he reached out and got his hand on the gun. He pushed himself up with his other hand and half-fell, half-turned so that he landed in a sitting position, facing the two women.

Only they weren't there anymore.

The noises of battle, the grunts of effort and the slap of fists against flesh and bone, told him that the fight had moved into the dining room. Dana and Joyce weren't saying anything now. They were using all their breath and energy to stay alive.

Toby caught hold of a table and pulled and pushed himself to his feet. Pain rippled up his left thigh and through his groin. He could tell he had pulled a muscle. He tried to take a tottering step, felt himself falling, caught himself on the back of the divan. Breathing hard, he pushed off and hobbled toward the door between the living room and the dining area.

He got there in time to see Joyce swing a broken chair leg at Dana's head. Dana went over backward onto the dining table and flung her legs out as she rolled to the other side. One foot caught Joyce on the shoulder and sent her staggering back against a china cabinet. The glass in the cabinet door shattered. More streaks of blood appeared on Joyce's blouse as the razor-sharp shards slashed her. She screamed.

Then she lunged forward, slid face-down across the table, and tackled Dana. Both women crashed to the floor on the far side of the table. Toby leaned against the side of the doorway, propping himself up as he watched and waited. Again he could hear the fight but couldn't see it.

They rolled out from behind the table, and now it wasn't a martial arts duel any longer. It was a hair-pulling, eye-gouging, no-holds-barred brawl. Dana rammed a knee into Joyce's midsection and then slugged her in the jaw. Joyce raked her fingernails down the side of Dana's face, clawing for her eyes. Dana jerked back, and that gave Joyce the chance to throw her off and roll away. Joyce grabbed up one of the broken chair legs and swung it, slamming it hard across Dana's back. Dana cried out. Joyce surged up onto her knees and lifted the chair leg again, poised to bring it down on Dana's head in a skull-crushing blow.

Toby shot her.

The automatic barely bucked in his hand as he fired. He remembered what Larry had said about head shots and bulletproof vests, but he knew Joyce wasn't wearing a vest because he could see her bra through her thin blouse. He aimed for her chest. The bullet went high, though, tearing through her throat instead and pitching her over backward. Blood spurted as she gurgled and thrashed and jerked for a few seconds. Then the reaction subsided and Joyce seemed to relax, almost as if she were lying down on her back to go to sleep. Toby lowered the gun.

Dana whimpered in pain. Toby looked at her, saw blood on her face and clothes. She wasn't as bloody as she had been after killing Hans on the front porch of the farm house, but then most of that blood had been his. The crimson smears on her now came from her blood.

"Dana!" Toby said. "Dana, are you all right?" He didn't know how much longer he could stay on his feet before his injured leg gave out again.

But one thing he was sure of: all the shooting in the past few minutes would have been heard and reported, and by this time, the cops were undoubtedly on their way.

It wouldn't be good if he and Dana were found here with a dead woman and half a million dollars in stolen money. Not good at all.

4.

Dana groaned and pushed herself to her feet. She slung her head, getting the tangled blond hair out of her eyes, and nearly fell. Her palms slapped against the highly polished wood of the dining room table as she caught herself.

"Joyce …?" she said.

"Dead," Toby told her.

"Are you—?"

"I'm hurt, but probably not as bad as you are. Dana, we've got to get out of here."

She nodded weakly. "I know." She took a deep breath. "That's my gun you've got, isn't it?"

"Yeah."

"We'll leave hers here."

She pushed herself away from the table at the same time Toby straightened from where he had been leaning against the door jamb. They staggered together, caught hold of each other. They would either knock each other down, or stand together.

They stayed on their feet. "The money's still in the Lexus," Dana said. "We have to move it."

"Why not just take Larry's car?"

"Once the cops come in here and take a look around, they'll put out a bulletin on the Lexus if it's gone. They won't know anything about the pickup, though."

She had a point. Even though they were shot up, beat up, and nearly out of time, they had to transfer the money. They stumbled toward the back of the house.

Later, Toby didn't know how they managed to do it. The whole thing was sort of blurry in his memory. All he knew was that he gritted his teeth against the pain and forced his leg to work as he carried canvas satchel after canvas satchel of cash from the Lexus to the pickup, tossing the bags into the back. Dana helped, but she was pale and quivering and barely able to stand, so she carried only a few bags. Toby worried that she was going to go into shock from loss of blood. She had a bullet wound in her right arm and another in her left side. He had no idea how serious they were, but from the looks of her, they must have been bad.

Finally, he got all the money transferred from the Lexus to the pickup. It must not have taken as long as he thought, because he didn't hear sirens approaching until he had finished the job. He opened the door and helped Dana into the passenger seat. No way she could drive. Even if she tried, she might pass out and wreck the pickup.

Toby hobbled back into the laundry room. Max and Clifford, spooked by all the gunfire and yelling earlier, were hiding behind the dryer. "Come on, guys," Toby said, his voice hoarse with strain. If the dogs didn't come right away, he would have to leave them. He didn't want to abandon them, but he wouldn't have any choice. Those sirens were only a few blocks away now.

The dogs poked their noses out and then came to him. He caught hold of their leashes and tugged them out to the pickup. They vaulted eagerly into the back of the vehicle.

"Bet this is the first time you guys have ridden around with half a million bucks," Toby said as he closed the back.

He had to hang on to the pickup as he made his way to the driver's door. He opened it and dragged himself up onto the seat, half collapsing onto it. Dana was slumped in the far corner, apparently unconscious. She had passed out, just as Toby had feared she might. He hoped that was all it was, hoped that she wasn't dead.

He was going to have to find his own way out of Dallas.

He started the pickup, put it in reverse, and backed out of the driveway, maneuvering onto the grassy strip that bordered it in order to get around Joyce's car. When he got to the street he turned the wheel and backed into it, thankful there was no traffic just then. He dropped the lever into Drive and gave the pickup some gas. It rolled forward, and as it did so, flashing lights appeared in the rearview mirror. But the cops were too late to see that the pickup had just left the house where they were headed. For all they knew he was just driving by innocently. He wanted them to keep thinking that, so he maintained a steady speed for a couple of blocks, then signaled a left turn and took it at a reasonable speed.

None of the police cars came after him.

5.

He heard later that the cops cordoned off the area and didn't let anybody in or out of a six-block radius for several hours. They had missed him by minutes.

That was long enough, though. Long enough for him to be able to put Dallas behind them, and he didn't care if he never came back.

Ten

1.

Toby found a highway that headed west and kept driving as long as he could. He wanted to put as much distance between them and the five killings as possible.

Out of Dallas and through Fort Worth, past endless strip malls and car dealerships and restaurants. Past big box discount stores and home improvement warehouses and electronics mega-stores. Through bumper-to-bumper seventy-mile-an-hour traffic.

And finally into open country again, with the coast-to-coast trucks on Interstate 20. Through Weatherford and on to the west.

They couldn't stop at a motel, not with Dana covered with blood the way she was. So as dusk settled down, Toby pulled the pickup into a rest area not far beyond the Brazos River. It overlooked a long valley stretching off to the north, with a stream at the bottom of it. Probably the same river, Toby thought as he leaned back against the seat and drew a deep breath.

Dana stirred. She had made a few noises and moved around enough times while he was driving so that he knew she was still alive, but she hadn't really regained consciousness. Now she moaned and her eyes fluttered open. "Wh-where are we?" she said.

"Take it easy," Toby said. "Don't worry about a thing, Dana. It's all right."

He wished that was true. Joyce's unexpected arrival at Larry's apartment had come close to ruining everything. Now they were both injured, Dana perhaps seriously, and although they seemed to have made a clean getaway, Toby wasn't going to be convinced of that until more time went by without the police coming after them.

But it wouldn't do any good to tell Dana all that, not with the shape she was in, so for now he would put up a brave front and just do the best he could. He had to hope that was enough.

The dogs started barking in the back. Toby said, "You just stay there and rest. I'll tend to the boys, and then we'll think about what we need to do next."

Dana mumbled agreement.

Toby opened the door and started to step out of the pickup. He had to grab on to the door to support himself as his left leg tried to give underneath him. It didn't hurt all that much anymore, but it was sure stiff and weak. His right leg was painful, too, from the gash on his knee. But the stain on that leg of his coveralls didn't look too bad, and he figured that in the fading light, no one else at the rest area would notice it.

He shut the door gently and limped to the back of the pickup. He got Max and Clifford out and walked them, gritting his teeth against the pain as he had to move a little faster than he wanted to in order to keep up with them. The rest area was full of new, intriguing smells—after all, thousands, maybe millions, of dogs had pissed and crapped here—and he had trouble tugging the two of them back to the pickup. Finally, he got them back into the vehicle.

It was almost full dark by now. The yellow sodium lights in the rest area were coming on. Toby got into the pickup and said, "If I get you a clean shirt from the back, can you put it on?"

"You'll have to help me," Dana said between gritted teeth.

"I will."

That took a while, despite their best efforts. Toby got the shirt and then helped Dana peel off the bloody one she was wearing. The blood had dried and the fabric was stuck to the wounds. Toby had to pull it loose, and that started the blood flowing again. He had picked a black shirt for Dana, though, in the hope that the stains wouldn't show as much. He had brought one of his shirts with him, too, and he tore strips off it to use as makeshift bandages. He wrapped them around her arm and torso and tied them tightly in place, then helped her struggle into the black shirt.

Dana was only half-conscious throughout and couldn't do much to help herself. Toby lifted her to finish getting the clean shirt on, then leaned her head back against the seat. He buttoned the shirt but didn't try to tuck it into her jeans. He said, "We'll find a motel somewhere. I don't think anybody will pay much attention to us now."

He got the pickup moving again, pulling onto the interstate and building up speed. He didn't know how close they were to the nearest town, but he hoped it wasn't far.

As it turned out, the next place to stop was a good thirty or forty miles away, and the distance seemed even farther to Toby. Finally, though, after going up a steep hill, a good-sized cluster of lights appeared along the right-hand side of the highway. The town was called Ranger, and Toby pulled over at the first cheap, undistinguished motel he came to.

He checked in, paying cash as usual, and drove the pickup along the lot to the unit, past a swimming pool with some shabby lawn furniture around it. A bored-looking couple sat there watching three yelling kids splash around in the water. The place was a little too well-lit for Toby's tastes, but they would have to make do, he told himself as he parked in front of the room. He unlocked the room door and swung it open, then hurried back to the pickup to help Dana.

If anybody asked, he was going to pretend to be drunk and act like Dana was, too. He didn't think anybody would question that. Even fancy motels got their share of drunken adulterers, and this one was far from fancy.

Nobody was around except the kids in the pool and their parents, and they didn't pay any attention as Toby put an arm around Dana and helped her from the pickup into the room. He used his foot to shut the door behind them and lowered her onto the foot of the bed. She was shivering now. Loss of blood, more than likely.

He started to take her shirt off so he could check on the wounds, but she stopped him. "Let me … rest a minute," she said. "Then we'll go in the bathroom … Easier to clean up any blood there." She managed to smile at him. "Get … the dogs … and our bags."

Toby nodded. Everything had to look as normal as possible. He did as Dana told him and brought in the dogs and the bags.

He left the half-million in the back of the truck. That made him a little nervous, but he didn't want to start lugging in money bags until later, when people around the motel were more likely to be asleep.

Dana looked a little stronger after resting for a few minutes. He helped her hobble into the bathroom. She sat on the toilet and he sat on the edge of the bathtub as he took her shirt off.

"Are you hit anywhere else?" he asked. "Anywhere below the waist?"

"No … sore down there where Joyce … kicked me … but no bullet holes."

He used warm water from the sink to soak off the strips of cloth he had tied around her wounds. Dana was frighteningly pale, and she winced and shivered harder as he uncovered the bullet holes. The one in her right arm was in the fleshy part of the upper arm, about three inches above the elbow. Toby saw both an entrance and an exit wound, and since Dana's arm wasn't flopping around loosely, he assumed the bone wasn't broken. The slug had passed straight through, taking some meat with it and leaving a wound that had bled heavily.

The wound in her side was similar. The bullet hadn't really penetrated, but instead had plowed a fairly deep furrow in the flesh below her left breast. Again, the injury had bled a lot, and Toby had no doubt it hurt like blazes. But it wasn't really as bad as it looked.

"I've got to clean these," he said.

Dana nodded. "I know."

"It'll sting."

"It'll be a lot worse than that, and you know it." She summoned up another weak smile.

Toby set to work. He didn't want to leave bloody towels behind, and he didn't want to draw attention by stealing towels, so he ripped up another shirt to use as rags. He could always buy more shirts. There was half a million dollars right outside in the pickup.

Of course, a lot of that money was earmarked already for saving Dana's life. He didn't need to lose sight of that fact.

She bit her lip and clutched the towel bar to keep from crying out as he cleaned the blood away from the wounds. When that was done, she said, "Go find a drugstore and get some alcohol, antibiotic cream, bandages, anything like that you can find. And cranberry juice."

"Cranberry juice?"

"It's … a natural antibiotic … might help keep infection from … setting in."

Toby nodded as he washed the blood off his hands. "I'll be back as quick as I can."

2.

By the time Toby got back to the motel room, Dana had crawled into the bathtub and gone to sleep. Only a little more blood had seeped from the wounds while he was gone. He woke her and helped her sit up. She whimpered in pain as he poured alcohol directly into the wounds, but even though her eyes rolled up in their sockets for a second, she didn't faint. She hung on stubbornly to consciousness.

"I'm in your hands, Toby," she murmured. "In your hands …"

"I won't let you down," he said.

He put antibiotic cream on gauze pads and bandaged them into place over the bullet holes in her arm. The wound in her side was more difficult, but he managed to get strips of gauze over it as well. He helped her to the bed and she sat on the end of it again. The waistband of her jeans was covered with dried blood on the left side. Toby took off her shoes, then unfastened the jeans and worked them down over her hips and pulled them off of her legs. He had already taken off her bra while he was working on the bullet wounds, so that left her clad only in panties. He got the blanket from the bed and wrapped it around her. It had been hot in the room when they arrived, because the air conditioner wasn't turned on. The room was still pretty warm as far as Toby was concerned, but Dana was freezing. He had to get some fluids in her to fight the dehydration.

He fetched ice from the machine down the sidewalk and filled one of the bathroom cups. He poured cranberry juice into it and held the cup to her lips. She drank greedily. He refilled the cup and she emptied it again. A faint tinge of color came back into her face.

The dogs sat in the corner and watched the whole thing, curious but subdued. They seemed to sense that serious business was going on. Or maybe he was giving them credit for too much intelligence. Maybe they were just calm because there was no food in sight.

"I've got to get you something to eat," Toby said. "There's a hamburger place just down the road. Will you be all right here for a few minutes?"

Dana nodded. "Turn the TV on before you go." Her voice was still weak, but not as much as it had been earlier.

Toby left the TV on one of the news channels and hurried on his errand. When he got back, he saw that Dana had scooted up to the head of the bed so that she could prop her back against it. She was still wrapped up tightly in the blanket.

"We're on the news again," she said.

"The armored truck robbery?"

"Yeah. Can you believe the cops haven't even found it yet?"

"If nobody saw Larry and me tow it into that garage, there's no reason for them to look in there." The truck might not be discovered until the stink of the dead bodies inside the garage drew attention from outside. That might be several days, maybe even longer. "What about the business at Larry's apartment?"

"You mean Joyce?" Dana said. "Nothing on the news about it. The police will be looking for Larry. A woman found dead in his apartment, especially a former girlfriend like that, he's bound to be the only suspect they have right now."

"His car's still there."

"They'll think he took off some other way."

That made sense. The cops would look for Larry, but just like the armored truck, it might be a long time before they found him.

Toby unwrapped the burgers he had brought back with him. Dana wasn't hungry, but he convinced her to eat, telling her that she needed the beef to help her replace some of the blood she had lost. She nibbled on a burger. The dogs wound up getting most of it.

After a while, she said, "What about your knee? You've never done anything about it."

"Hasn't been time."

"Take those coveralls off and come over here."

He grinned. "Man, I hope we both feel better the next time you say something like that."

3.

She wanted to fuss over him and take care of him, but she was just too weak for that. He cleaned the cut on his knee and let her help him bandage it. That at least made her feel like she was accomplishing something. Then she lay back and dozed off and left him watching the news on TV.

After a while he switched over to a channel showing music videos.

Dana slept peacefully, but Toby was too wired to even feel drowsy. He watched TV until midnight, then went outside to the pickup and started bringing in the money bags, being quiet and careful about it. Both legs hurt, but he ignored the pain. He wanted to see that cash for himself.

The room had only one small table and one chair. He stacked the bags on the floor beside the table, sat down in the chair, and started unloading them. The bills were all sorted and banded, so he was able to arrange them in different piles according to denomination without any trouble. There were rolled coins, too, so he sorted them as well. When he was finished, he had quite an impressive-looking mountain of money on the table.

He started counting it.

When he reached four hundred thousand, quite a bit was still uncounted. He grinned and kept on with what he was doing. When he passed five hundred thousand and kept counting, he knew that Larry had underestimated the take.

It was nearly two in the morning when he finished. He got a piece of motel stationery and a motel pen and wrote down the total so he wouldn't forget it: $649,237.55. Enough to pay off Gary and Walt and have nearly a quarter of a million left over. His hand shook a little as he wrote the numbers. He had never seen that much money before in his life. Had never even dreamed of having that much. Bounced from foster family to foster family, all of them struggling because, let's face it, none of them would have taken in a loser who'd been abandoned by his mother unless they really needed the money. Those thoughts whirled through his brain, chasing the numbers he wrote on the paper.

He looked over at the bed and wanted to wake Dana and tell her. She was sleeping so peacefully, though, that he couldn't bring himself to disturb her. After everything she had gone through today, she really needed her rest.

Toby put the money back in the bags and left them in the floor beside the table. Then he stretched out on the bed beside Dana and turned off the light. He listened to her breathing and thought about the money, and it was a long time before he went to sleep.

4.

In the morning, Dana had him repack the money in their suitcases. Then he went down the street to the drugstore where he had bought the supplies the previous evening and bought a box of black trash bags. They put the clothes and other things from their suitcases in a couple of the trash bags. The canvas satchels, emptied and flattened, went into another bag. Toby loaded everything in the pickup. He didn't say anything about it, but he could tell that Dana was irritated with him because he had brought the money in and counted it while she slept.

Surprisingly, considering the fact that it was a dump in most other respects, the motel offered a "continental breakfast". Toby walked over to the lobby and got coffee, bagels, donuts, a couple of bananas. He carried them back to the room.

While they were sitting on the bed and eating, it finally got the best of him. "I didn't take any of it," he said. "It's all still there, and it's a lot more than we thought it would come to."

Dana was still weak, but her color was a lot better and so was her appetite. She put down the bagel in her hand and looked at Toby. "I never thought you stole any of it," she said. "I was just worried that somebody saw you carrying in those money bags."

"The cops aren't knocking on our door, are they? I thought it was late enough so that nobody would notice, and as far as I can see, they didn't."

"Maybe you were just lucky."

"What's wrong with that?"

"Larry always relied on his luck. Eventually it ran out."

"Well, mine's got a long way to go. Look how lucky I was to have met you."

She shook her head. "I don't know about that."

"I do." He reached over and took her hand. "I'm sorry about the money. I know you know a lot more about this sort of stuff than I do. I'll wait and talk to you before I do anything like that again."

She nodded and squeezed his hand. "Okay." After a moment, she went on, "I'd say that you'll learn as you go along, but ... I don't want you to learn, Toby. I don't want you to be a criminal. This has got to be the end of it for you."

"Yeah?" He frowned. "I hadn't really thought about it. What *am* I going to do now?"

"Your share of the money would put you through college. You can go to school and do anything you want to with your life from here on out."

"You think so? I don't know ... I always hated school. Did okay on my grades, I guess, but I never liked it. Everybody there was so stupid and shallow, not interested in anything except their own little social circle. God, I hated those bastards."

"College isn't like that."

"Did you go?"

"No, but—"

"I'll bet it is. I'll bet it's just like high school, only worse."

"What are you going to do, then, if you don't go to college?"

"Hang with you?"

"I'm twenty years older than you, Toby. Twice your age."

"Yeah, well, in twenty more years you'll only be a third older than me. See, I can do math. If we stay together long enough, eventually we'll be the same age."

She laughed. "Don't think the idea doesn't sound appealing. Sooner or later, though, it's going to matter to you. Take my word for it."

"We'll deal with that when the time comes. Right now I don't want to be anywhere else, or with anybody else."

She leaned closer to him and raised her left arm. The right was too stiff from the bullet wound for her to be able to move it much. She touched his cheek and said quietly, "You really are a sweet boy." Her lips pressed against his. He put his arms around her, gingerly.

"When we both feel better, I'm going to make love to you for a week," he said.

"I'll hold you to that."

It was only later that he realized he had thought of it as making love, rather than fucking her.

5.

They didn't get in any hurry to check out. Dana wanted to wait until most of the other guests at the motel had moved on before she and Toby left. While they were waiting, he changed the bandages on her wounds and cleaned them again. The crease in her side was in good shape and looked as if it had already started to heal. The holes in her arm were redder and a little puffy. Toby put a lot of the antibiotic cream on the pads he used to cover them.

"You ought to be taking some real antibiotics," he said.

"Yeah, so you know any crooked doctors?"

"Don't you know anybody like that? Maybe some guy who lost his medical license because he performed surgery while he was drunk or high and accidentally killed somebody?"

She laughed. "That's only in comic books and movies. You did as good a job of patching me up as anybody I know could have. Say, maybe that's what you should do."

"What?"

"Become a doctor. Maybe you've got a natural talent for it."

Toby just stared at her for a second and then shook his head. The idea of him becoming a doctor ... well, it was crazy, that was all there was to it.

They finished loading the pickup and checked out a little later. The girl working in the office paid only scant attention as Toby dropped the room key on the counter and left it there. Nobody at the motel would remember them. They were just two drops in the endlessly flowing stream of humanity on the interstate, with nothing to distinguish them from thousands of other travelers.

Except, of course, for the gunshot wounds, and the six hundred thousand dollars in the back of the pickup ...

Dana couldn't drive, the shape she was in, so Toby stayed behind the wheel. His legs were still sore from their various injuries, but they were better today. As they passed the exit for some place called Cross Plains, Toby asked, "Where are we going?"

"Yeah, I suppose it's time we started thinking about that," Dana said. "Yesterday, the only thing that was important was getting out of Dallas."

"That's pretty much what I thought, too. I just headed west because that's the way the road went."

"It's as good a direction as any, maybe better. Not as many towns out this direction, which means fewer cops. We need to find a place to wait for a while."

"What about calling Gary and Walt?"

She shook her head. "Not yet. Not as beat up as we are. I need to heal and get some of my strength back before I face them, just in case there's trouble. I hope there won't be ... I hope they'll just take the money and leave us alone ... but you never know."

"That Joyce, she was with them?"

"That's what I heard."

"But she came to Larry's apartment by herself."

"Larry called her, remember? He probably told her not to tell Gary and Walt. Larry could always get Joyce to do whatever he wanted her to do. I don't think that would change just because they weren't together anymore. He could talk her around to anything."

"He couldn't persuade you to go to bed with both of them, though."

She looked over at him with a frown. "How do you know about that?"

"He told me some stuff, while we were in the wrecker."

"What kind of stuff?"

"Stuff about you and guys, mostly."

Dana said, "Huh. He was just jealous, I guess, because I wouldn't ever do anything with him."

"You mean he made it all up?"

"I don't know exactly what he said, but probably not. I've done some pretty wild things, and I don't deny it. You live like I did, the people I lived around, you do some stuff that maybe, normally, you'd never even think about doing. There's always a lot of drugs and sex around." She shrugged. "I didn't like drugs."

"But you liked sex."

"I still do. I've settled down some, though. And there hasn't been much of an opportunity for a long time ..."

"Uh, did you and my mother ever ..."

She looked over at him again. "Oh, my God. Are you serious?"

Toby suddenly felt uncomfortable and wished he hadn't brought it up. "I'm sorry, I just thought—"

"I'll let you in on a secret, Toby. Despite male fantasies to the contrary, not every woman likes to fool around with other women. Some of us don't have any desire to eat pussy."

"Okay, okay. Can we just drop the subject?"

"Sure. You need to remember, though, that what's past is past. What counts is now."

"Yeah. I'll remember."

They drove on. Abilene, Sweetwater, Big Spring, all fell behind them. The highway climbed a gentle incline that Dana pointed out and said was called the Cap Rock, the edge of the vast plateau that formed the rest of West Texas. It didn't seem like much of a landmark to Toby. They got lunch at a Dairy Queen in some little town beside the interstate. Toby never saw a sign telling him the name of the place. Then on into the sprawl of Midland and Odessa, where the air stunk of the oil refineries that dotted the landscape and sometimes shouldered right up next to the highway. Signs of the oil industry were everywhere now, drilling rigs, pumping stations, storage tanks. Some of the equipment was rusting from disuse, evidence that the oil business wasn't what it had once been. But it was still there, inescapable once a certain point had been passed.

Late in the afternoon, as they neared a town called Monahans, Toby saw large, seemingly endless, rolling hills of sand off to the north of the highway. The sand hills paralleled the road for a while and then disappeared. Toby had never seen anything like them.

The next town was Pecos. Toby had heard of it before, and after a minute, he remembered why, connecting it with stories about Judge Roy Bean. Cowboy stuff. The law west of the Pecos. He had never cared much for things like that.

But as they approached the town, he looked off into the southwest and saw something in the far distance that made him sit up straighter on the pickup seat. "What's that?" he asked, pointing.

"Where?"

"Over there on the horizon. Where the sun's going down."

Dana smiled. "Toby ... those are mountains."

"Well, I'll be damned," he said.

For the first time in his life, he was seeing mountains. Real mountains.

"Let's find a motel in Pecos," Dana said. "I'm tired, and this is as good a place as any."

Eleven

1.

The motel was a fairly nice one beside the interstate. Toby had put several hundred dollars in his wallet when he transferred the money from the satchels to the suitcases that morning, so he paid in cash and told the desk clerk that he and his wife might be staying for several days. Seeing how young Toby was, the clerk asked, "Are you on your honeymoon?"

"That's right," Toby said. Once the story got around, if anybody saw him limping they would probably think he had hurt himself with some bedroom gymnastics. In a way, the lie drew attention to them, but it might also make everyone around the motel more willing to overlook any oddities about their stay.

The room was on the back side of the motel. Toby drove the pickup around there and helped Dana inside. He unloaded while she rested.

"There's a discount store just up the street," she told him. "After supper, go over there and buy a couple more suitcases. It looks a little strange carrying garbage bags in and out of the room."

"Okay. What do you want to eat?"

"I'd love some pizza."

"I saw a sign for a pizza place. What do you want on it, everything?"

"No anchovies or bell peppers. Anything else is fine."

"Okay. I'll be back when I've gotten everything done," he said.

She was sitting in a wing chair turned so that it faced the television. She took the little automatic from her pocket and put it beside her in the chair so that it would be easy to get to. "I'll be here," she said.

2.

They stayed at the motel for a week, letting their injuries heal, before Dana was ready to make a move. By the end of that time, the pulled muscle in Toby's left leg was fine again, and the scab had come off the gash on his right knee, leaving only a thin, pale scar. Dana had been hurt worse, though, and wasn't in such good shape. Continued application of alcohol and antibiotic cream had kept the crease in her side from getting infected. The holes in her arm remained red and sore for several days, but finally they began to heal, too. The arm was still stiff, though, and Toby was afraid if she had to use it too much, she might injure it again.

They watched a lot of TV and read the newspapers he brought to the room. A small story in the Dallas *Morning News* mentioned that a young woman named Kelly Brannon had been found by police after escaping from several men who had kidnapped and assaulted her over a period of two days. She was in the hospital, in serious condition, and hadn't been able to give the police any good leads to her abductors.

So she had made it out alive somehow. That was a surprise, but Toby was glad to read about it.

Six days after the robbery, the armored car and the wrecker were found in the garage, along with the bodies of the three guards. Nothing was said in any of the stories about Larry's body.

That worried Toby. "What if he didn't die? Maybe he came to and got out of there."

Dana shook her head. "As bad as he was wounded, he should have been dead within minutes after we left."

Woulda, shoulda, coulda. They should have put a couple of bullets in Larry's head just to make sure. Dana was the pro at this sort of thing, though.

But even pros could make a mistake now and then.

"Besides," Dana went on, "my guess is that his body was there, but the cops haven't released that information yet. They always hold things back. They identified Larry's body, connected it with Joyce's body being found at Larry's apartment, and they're still investigating, trying to figure out exactly what happened."

That made sense. Still, Toby would have felt better if he knew for certain that Larry was dead.

After the week was up, Dana was ready to contact Gary and Walt. She had Toby buy a prepaid long-distance calling card. "The calls are routed through different computers scattered around the country," she explained. "The company has a lot of them, which makes calls through them hard to trace. They show up on Caller ID as coming from different area codes, and they're never the same twice in a row. And the area code is never the same as the one you're really calling from."

"How do you know shit like that?" Toby said.

"You have to learn a little bit of everything if you want to stay alive."

Once she had the calling card, she placed a call to a bar in Chicago. "Is Jack Turner tending bar there this afternoon?" she asked. After a moment she said, "Well, then, tell him Linda called, will you? Thanks." She hung up.

"Ooh," Toby said. "Secret code."

She gave him a look. "That's right. People engaged in illegal activities tend to be pretty secretive about where they are and what they're doing."

"Yeah, but you got to admit it's a little silly."

"We'll see," she said.

Twenty minutes later, she placed another call, identified herself as Carmen, and then wrote down a number on the pad of paper next to the phone. She hung up without saying thanks this time.

"That wasn't very friendly," Toby said.

"There was nobody on the other end but a voice-activated machine. It gave me the number I need."

"Really? That'll get you through to those guys?"

"We can hope," Dana said. She took a deep breath and punched in the digits of the phone number she had written down.

Toby was sitting on the edge of the bed. He leaned forward and felt himself getting tense as they waited for somebody to answer the call. After several rings, which he could faintly hear as burring sounds, he heard the click as the phone on the other end was picked up. He heard a man's voice but couldn't make out the words.

"Hello, Gary," Dana said. "It's me."

Her face was pale, and Toby knew the pallor was caused by strain, since her natural color had returned during the week of recuperation. He figured he might be a little washed-out himself.

"Yes, I'm alive," Dana said after a moment. "That shouldn't come as any surprise to you … No, I didn't have anything to do with that. That was all Larry's idea … It's the truth, Gary. He's the one who pulled the double-cross and stole all that money …" Her hand tightened on the phone. "I don't really give a fuck if you believe me or not."

Toby grimaced as he clenched and unclenched his hands. He wanted to tell Dana that talking to the guy that way might not be a good idea, but he kept quiet. She had told him before she placed the call that she didn't want the others knowing about him just yet.

"Here's what I want to do," she said, cutting into the angry buzz of words from the other end of the connection. "I want to pay you and

Walt ... That's right, the whole four hundred grand ... Because I'd rather pay you and have the two of you off my back, that's why ... Roy and Hans? I don't know a thing about it ... Really? I guess that's a break for me, then ... Four hundred thousand, that's right. You and Walt split it any way you want, that's none of my concern, just as long as you both agree to leave me alone from now on ... I told you, I don't care if you believe me, I just want you to take the money ... Sure, talk it over. I'll call you back in, what, fifteen minutes? Sure."

She put the phone down, reached up and wiped sweat off her forehead.

"Well?" Toby said. "What did he say?"

"He didn't believe me. He still thinks I'm the one who double-crossed everybody after the job in San Antonio. But he seemed pretty interested when I said that about paying them off. If all they really want is the money, that's about the best we can hope for."

"You're still not worried they'll want revenge?"

Her mouth twisted. "I guess I'll always worry about that a little. But I really believe they'll leave me alone after this."

Toby took a deep breath. "Well, then, we'll hope they go along with it."

The fifteen minutes Dana waited before placing another call was a long time to the two of them. Toby stood up and paced back and forth a few times before he noticed her glaring at him. "Sorry," he said as he sat down on the bed again. "I guess I'm just nervous."

"So am I. There's a lot riding on this."

Their whole future, however long it might be. That was all.

Dana picked up the phone and punched in the numbers.

When it was answered, she said, "Hello, Walt. I figured it would be you I talked to this time ... I'm glad to hear that. Are you sure? I don't want anybody backing out of the deal ..." She caught Toby's eye and gave him a nod. He clenched his fists and grinned. "You pick the time, I'll pick the place," she went on. "I'll call back tomorrow. Deal?"

She nodded again as the man on the other end of the line spoke firmly.

"Deal," she said and then hung up.

"Yes!" Toby said. "They bought it."

"They didn't have to buy it. I didn't tell them anything but the truth."

"Now what?"

"Now we go sight-seeing."

3.

"I never liked cowboy stuff," Toby said. "I grew up around too many goat-ropers in Oklahoma."

He wiped sweat off his forehead as they walked around the sidewalks of downtown Pecos, such as it was, several blocks north of the interstate. The heat seemed to bother Dana, too, but she endured it stoically. "Up there," she said, pointing to an old building on their left.

"West of the Pecos Museum and Orient Saloon," Toby read off the sign. "Does that mean we can get a drink there?"

"No, the saloon's part of the museum. I read about it on a brochure at the motel. It's been restored so that it looks like it did in frontier days."

"Yippee," Toby said.

Dana frowned at him. "We're not here to learn about Old West history. Just settle down."

Toby was about to say, "Yes, Mom," when he decided that probably wouldn't be a good idea. Might stir up too many unpleasant memories for both of them.

The museum and the restored saloon were fairly busy, since they represented the town's only real tourist attractions. As Toby watched the people coming and going, he realized why Dana was interested in the place. She had to meet Gary and Walt in some public location, where they wouldn't want to start shooting or cause any other trouble. The museum fit the bill.

They spent an hour going through the old saloon and wound up out in back of it, where a grave was surrounded by a low, red brick fence. Toby read the inscription off the simple headstone. "Robert Clay Allison, 1840-1887. He never killed a man that did not need killing." He paused. "Words to live by."

"You could do worse," Dana said.

"Yeah, I guess." He looked over at her. "You really believe in all this stuff, don't you?"

"Let's go," she said without answering his question.

4.

Dana called Walt and Gary the next day, and when one of them answered, she said, "The West of the Pecos Museum, in Pecos, Texas." After a moment, she nodded. "All right. I'll be there." She hung up.

She looked worried. Toby asked, "What's wrong?"

"Walt set the time at two o'clock tomorrow afternoon."

"So?"

"So they must be pretty close."

"Not necessarily," Toby said. "You can get a flight into Dallas-Fort Worth from almost anywhere in the country, and that's only a seven or eight hour drive from here."

"Yeah, I suppose you're right." She didn't look totally convinced, though, and he wondered exactly what her instincts were telling her.

He patted the bed beside him and said, "Come here."

"Toby, I'm not in the mood."

"You don't have to be in the mood for anything. I just want you to sit beside me for a minute."

She got up from the chair and crossed the motel room to sit beside him on the end of the bed. He slipped his arm around her, being careful not to put any pressure on the wound in her side.

"Listen, it's all going to be all right," he said. "We've come this far, accomplished this much. We've got over half a million dollars. We're going to use it to get you out of this mess, and we're going to use what's left to start a new life."

"I've told you, you're not going to want to spend the rest of your life with me."

"Let's worry about that when it gets here. In the meantime, don't borrow trouble. Everything's going to be all right."

"How do you know that?"

"Hey, you may be the big hotshot bank robber and professional criminal, but I've got pretty good survival instincts, too, you know. I managed to make it through some pretty rough times, and I did okay for myself. My gut tells me this is going to go just fine."

"If your gut is wrong, we could wind up dead."

"Everybody does, sooner or later."

"Well, that's true." She leaned against him and rested her head on his shoulder. After a moment, she said in a quiet voice, "I'm not ready for it to be over, though. Not now."

"Neither am I."

She turned her head, tilted her face to his. He kissed her. Banged up as they had been after leaving Dallas, they hadn't touched each other this way in over a week. But as soon as their lips met, the same urgency was still there.

Toby undressed her carefully. Her arm and her side were still bandaged. He got his clothes off and stretched out on the bed. He would have to let her set the pace, but that was all right. She straddled him, took his hard penis inside her, and settled down to rock slowly back and forth. She braced herself with her hands on his chest.

Going slow like that, it lasted a surprisingly long time. When they came, it was a soft, sweet moment of release, not the sort of thundering gallop they had experienced in the past.

If this *was* the last time, it wasn't a bad way to go out.

5.

The next day dawned clear, and the air was hot by nine o'clock in the morning. Toby got breakfast for them, walked the dogs, and tidied up the motel room. After spending over a week there, it was a little messy, not like a home got messy, but not the sort of sterile environment you usually found in a motel room. It looked lived in.

But not after today, not by them, anyway. One way or another, they would be gone from Pecos by nightfall.

Check-out time was eleven o'clock. Toby packed the pickup while Dana checked over their guns. He put the two suitcases containing the four hundred thousand right inside the back so they would be easy to get to. All they had to do was hand over the money to Gary and Walt and drive away.

Actually, Dana would do the handing over. The plan she had worked out called for Toby to pretend not to know her while they were at the museum. He would already be there playing tourist when she arrived. That way he could cover her without Gary and Walt knowing who he was, just in case of trouble.

When Toby went to check out, the same clerk was on duty who had been there when he checked in. The guy smiled and said, "Did you and your wife enjoy your stay?"

"Oh, yeah. Everything was fine."

"I'm not sure what you found to do in Pecos for over a week. It's not much of a town."

"We like it. Thinking of moving here, in fact."

"Is that so? Me, I'd like to get out." He was young, Hispanic, with a restless look in his dark eyes. "There's got to be more exciting places than this."

"Take it from me," Toby said. "Excitement's not all it's cracked up to be."

With a wave, he left the motel office and walked out to the pickup where Dana was waiting. He climbed in and drove off.

They still had some time to kill since the meeting with Gary and Walt wasn't until two o'clock. It was too hot to leave the dogs shut up in the pickup, so they had to drive around most of the time, stopping for lunch at an old-fashioned drive-in with awnings over the parking spaces for shade and carhops who brought the food. They were all Hispanic high school girls, and Toby admired their sleek brown legs in the shorts they wore.

"See?" Dana said. "You're interested in girls closer to your own age. That's the way it ought to be."

"There's not a one of them I'd rather have than you." He sipped some of the milkshake he had bought to go with his cheeseburger. "I'm perfectly happy."

Dana looked over at him. "Really?"

"Really." He meant it, too.

They lingered at the drive-in. It was still hot, even in the shade, but a light breeze that blew through the open windows of the pickup made it bearable. The drive-in was on Pecos's main downtown street, about four blocks from the museum. At one-thirty, Toby opened the door.

"You're sure about this?" he asked before he stepped out. "You haven't driven in over a week."

"I can handle it. My side's fine, and the arm's just a little stiff now."

"Okay. I'll wander down to the museum, then." He dropped to the asphalt parking lot of the drive-in and shut the pickup door.

The revolver he now thought of as his was in his pocket as he walked down the street toward the museum. A couple of times during the week they had spent in Pecos, he had driven out into the country, well away from town, and done some target shooting. The revolver felt very comfortable in his hand now, and most of the time he hit whatever he aimed at.

He did a quick count as he went into the museum. Eight people, all touristy looking, three kids and five adults. No sign of Gary and Walt. Dana had described them to him well enough so that he was confident he would know them. Gary was the taller of the two, skinny, with blond hair. Walt was shorter, stockier, with graying dark hair cut short. Both were able to blend into a crowd, but the museum was far from crowded today. Still, enough people were here so that Toby didn't think anybody would be tempted to start shooting. That was all that mattered.

He lingered at the polished mahogany bar where the cowboys who came to the Orient Saloon in the old days were once served. Off to his right was a staircase leading up to the second floor. He and Dana had checked it out the day before. The rooms up there had various historical displays in them. It would have been more accurate if some of the displays had said something about all the fucking of saloon girls that had gone on up there. Maybe a photo montage of the results of the diseases they passed on to their customers. Probably wouldn't do much for tourism, though.

He shifted his attention to the backbar and looked at all the vintage whiskey bottles lined up there. There was a gilt-edged mirror above the bottles, and that was how he was able to see Gary and Walt as they walked into the restored saloon.

He knew who they were right away. They matched Dana's descriptions perfectly, and they didn't even try to hide the fact that they were together. Toby rested his hands on the bar and put a stupid grin on his face, like he was just another dumb tourist. He thought about pretending to order a sarsaparilla from an imaginary bartender, but he decided that would be pushing the act. Dressed like he was in jeans and an untucked t-shirt, with sunglasses and a baseball cap on his head, they would glance at him and then ignore him.

Their mistake, if they tried anything funny.

They poked around the museum, acting like tourists, too. In fact, they struck Toby as seeming a little gay. He wondered about that. He knew they had hooked up with Joyce Sanders. Was it like a threesome thing, where they fooled around with her and each other? Toby bet himself that it was.

Dana came in, wearing jeans and a dark blue, short-sleeved top. She had on sunglasses, too, but she pushed them up on her hair as she stepped into the museum. The bandage wrapped around her arm was partially visible under the short sleeve but not too obvious. She looked around, spotted Gary and Walt, and smiled as if she had just encountered a pair of old friends. Which in a way she had, Toby supposed.

"Hi, guys," she said in a normal tone of voice. "Enjoying your trip?"

"We sure are," Gary said. "How about you?"

"Oh, it's been fine so far. I've had a great time seeing all the sights."

"Yeah," Walt said. He didn't bother trying not to look a little surly.

"Picked up any souvenirs?"

"As a matter of fact, I got some beautiful Navajo rugs over in New Mexico. They're right outside in the truck. You want to go take a look at them?"

"Hey, might as well." Gary looked around the saloon and shrugged. "I think we've seen enough in here."

Toby drifted toward the door as the three of them went out. He stopped at a countertop rack of postcards where he could watch through the window as Dana led the two men over to the pickup. It was parked at a meter on the street, about twenty yards to the right of the museum entrance.

His jaw tightened a little as Dana went behind the pickup to open the rear door of the camper top. Things had worked out so that he couldn't see her very well from here. But he could still see Gary and Walt as they stood on the sidewalk. He kept his eyes on them, waiting for Dana to hand them the suitcases full of money. Once that was done, they could walk away, and he could go outside, join Dana, and they would drive away, putting Pecos and the whole sorry mess behind them forever.

One of the tourists came up behind Toby. He heard the footstep and started to move over, thinking that whoever it was wanted to look at the postcards. "Sorry," he said.

The voice that replied was hoarse, but he recognized it anyway.

"That's all right, Junior," Larry said.

Twelve

1.

It took every bit of Toby's self-control not to yell in alarm and spin around. A shudder went through him. His hands gripped the edge of the glass counter where the postcard rack was located.

"That's right," Larry said. "Nice and quiet."

The blond teenager working behind the counter drifted toward them. "Can I help you?" she asked.

"No thanks," Larry said. "My friend and I are just looking."

"Well, if you need any help, y'all let me know."

"We sure will."

The girl started to turn away, but then she stopped and looked past Toby at Larry. "Are you all right, sir?"

Toby wanted to shout, *No, he's not all right! He's a crazy killer!*

But he didn't say anything, and Larry just chuckled and said, "Yeah, I'm fine. Just a little too much sun, maybe."

For the first time, Toby glanced over his shoulder. Larry was pale and haggard, still showing the effects of being shot a couple of times less than two weeks earlier. But considering that he ought to look dead, he was in pretty good shape.

The girl smiled and said, "Okay," then moved off down the counter to wait on one of the tourists.

Larry said to Toby, "You're doing just fine, Junior. Funny, I don't hear you complaining about being called that now."

"What do you want?" Toby asked.

"I think you know. And I'm going to get it, too. Look out there."

Toby felt his heart start to pound even faster as he saw Walt and Gary on the sidewalk with Dana. Walt had hold of her uninjured arm and was steering her along the sidewalk toward a van that was parked a couple of spaces behind the pickup. They were being careful enough so that nobody was likely to notice that anything was wrong, but they weren't giving her any choice in the matter, either.

"They're in it with you," Toby said.

"Of course they are. When I told them that Dana was setting up a trap for them and planned to kill them, they went right along with everything I said."

Toby thought about yelling that a woman was being kidnapped

outside. But if he did, Larry would probably shoot him, then Gary and Walt would kill Dana, and they would all take their chances on getting away with the money. That much was worth taking a risk—and so was revenge.

Even though no guns were in sight, Toby was sure all three of the men were armed. All he could do for the moment was play along. He took a deep breath and said in as normal a tone of voice as he could manage, "Why don't we go outside? I think I've seen everything there is to see in here."

"That's a good idea. You first."

Toby opened the museum door and stepped out onto the sidewalk. As he did so, Dana glanced back and saw him. She saw Larry, too, as he emerged from the building. Her eyes widened in surprise.

No one was near them on the sidewalk. As the museum door swung closed behind them, Toby said, "We should have put a bullet or two through your head, just to be sure."

"That would have been too quick. Dana's such a bitch she would have wanted me to suffer. Anyway, she came close enough to killing me, boy."

"Evidently not."

Larry grunted. Toby couldn't tell if he was angry or amused. He said, "Go down there and get in the van."

"What if I don't? You're going to shoot me in broad daylight, in the middle of town?"

"I shot those two guards in broad daylight on the side of a busy interstate, remember?"

Toby remembered, all right. He started toward the van.

As he came even with the pickup, with Larry close behind him, Max suddenly appeared behind the window in the side of the camper top and started barking. Even through the glass the sound was loud and startling. Toby sensed as much as saw from the corner of his eye how Larry's head jerked in that direction, and as Larry moved, so did Toby, without thinking about it.

He swung around to his right and brought his elbow up and smashed it into Larry's jaw. Larry was thrown sideways against the pickup. Max barked even louder and acted like he wanted to come right through the glass and rip Larry's throat out.

That wasn't a bad idea. Toby's hand shot out and grabbed Larry around the neck. He saw Larry's hand come out of his pants pocket with a gun in it, but before Larry could bring the weapon up, Toby smashed his head against the side of the camper. Larry dropped the gun and went limp. Toby gave him a hard shove that sent him sprawling on the sidewalk.

He hadn't heard any shots from Walt and Gary, but he didn't know what they were doing to Dana. Now as he spun in that direction he saw Dana snap a kick to Walt's knee that made the stocky man stagger back and drop into a pained crouch. Gary was slumped against the van, also in pain. It got worse a second later as Dana kicked him in the balls. As Gary screamed and fell to his knees, Dana broke into a run toward the pickup.

Toby had the door open already. He threw himself behind the wheel and jammed the key into the ignition. The motor started with a roar as he cranked it. Larry moved around a little on the sidewalk, but he was still too stunned to know what was going on, let alone to do anything about it.

In the side mirror, Toby saw Walt pull a gun. Toby twisted on the seat, stuck his arm out the window with the revolver in his hand, and pulled the trigger as Dana darted behind the pickup. The bullet ricocheted off the sidewalk near Walt and sent him diving for cover behind the van. Dana jerked the passenger door open and piled in, shouting, "Go!"

With the dogs barking frantically in the rear of the pickup, Toby twisted the wheel and gunned the engine. The left front fender of the pickup scraped the right rear fender of the car parked in front of the pickup as they shot out into the street. Toby spun the wheel again, careening left into a side street just past the museum. He went right and then left again and found himself headed west on one of the town's main streets. He saw a turn-off on the left for State Highway 17 and slid into it. He didn't know where he was going, but as long as it was away from Larry, Walt, and Gary, it was all right with him.

There were also the cops to worry about, but that seemed relatively minor at the moment. Although given the fact that he had shot off a gun on one of Pecos's main streets, they might be more inclined to use deadly force if they tried to stop him.

"Slow down a little," Dana said, maybe thinking the same thing. "I doubt if anybody back there got our license number, and the witnesses will probably give the cops half a dozen different descriptions of the pickup."

"Yeah, but we've got dark blue paint on the fender where we scraped that car," Toby said as he eased off the gas but didn't hit the brake. "They could identify us by that."

"I didn't say stop. I just meant don't drive like a bat out of hell. That attracts attention, too."

"You think Larry and the others are after us?"

Dana shook her head. "They all had unregistered guns, and some of the people in the museum might have been able to tell that they were trying to abduct us. I think they'll get out of Pecos as fast as they can."

"And then what?"

"I don't have any answers," Dana said. "For them or for us."

2.

The interstate went over the state highway just west of town. Toby could have gotten back on the freeway and headed west, toward El Paso, but Dana told him to keep going south.

"What's this way?" he asked.

"The Davis Mountains."

He could see them again in the distance, rugged and gray, a few of them wearing white caps of snow even during the summer. "The mountains," he said quietly.

They drove on. Toby gradually increased their speed once they were out of town. He watched the mirrors closely but didn't see any signs of pursuit from either the police or Larry, Walt, and Gary.

"What the hell happened?" he said after a while. "We had everything worked out."

"Larry," Dana said. "He ruined everything, and he shouldn't have even been alive. Did he say anything to you? Did he tell you how he got Gary and Walt to go along with him?"

"He said that he told them you were setting up a trap for them and intended to kill them. And they believed him."

"Damn!" Dana struck her thigh with a fist. "They knew Roy and Hans were dead. Larry probably told them I set that up, too. And Joyce is dead, and I put a couple of bullets into Larry ... No wonder they believed him! He made it look like I've been trying to wipe out everybody connected with that San Antonio job!"

Toby nodded. "Yeah, that makes sense. He's covering his tracks again."

"I should have listened to you, Toby. You were right. I don't know how Larry lived through those wounds, but he did it somehow. I guess he's just too ... too evil to die."

"Yeah, maybe. You think they'll come after us?"

Dana didn't hesitate with her answer. "Oh, yeah. We've still got the money, and now Gary and Walt think I'm trying to kill them. They'll come after us in self-defense." She thought about it for a moment and then went on, "Larry probably told them that I planned the armored car job in Dallas, and that I came to him for help with it instead of the other way around. Then I double-crossed him and tried to kill him so we could have all the money. To Gary and Walt, it'll all sound perfectly logical. Staying teamed up with Larry will make sense to them."

"Gary and Walt," Toby said. "Are those guys gay?"

"What?"

"Are they gay? They struck me a little that way, you know, back there in the museum. What little I saw of them."

Dana leaned her head against the seat and laughed. It was a tired, almost humorless sound. "Is everything about sex to you? They want to kill us, and you want to know if they're gay."

"Hey, I was just curious. I knew they were hooked up with that Joyce girl, and I thought it might be, like, a threesome."

"To tell you the truth, Toby, I really don't know. You can ask them, though, when we see them again. Because unless we're very lucky, I think we *will* see them again."

3.

They passed a couple of small communities as the state highway continued south toward the mountains. Mostly Hispanic, judging by the fact that the signs in front of the churches were all in Spanish. To Toby, it seemed that the mountains were just as far away as ever, but finally, he began to be able to tell that they were getting closer.

He saw an overpass ahead and realized they were coming to another highway. "That's I-ten," Dana said when he pointed it out to her. "Runs from El Paso to San Antonio and on over to Houston. We'll make a little jog on it and then turn south again toward Fort Davis. I think that's the best place for us to head right now."

"A fort?"

"That's the name of a little town in a valley that runs up into the mountains. There was a fort there once, a long time ago. Back when there were still Indians around here."

"But there aren't any soldiers there now?"

Dana shook her head. "No, no soldiers. Just tourists. There are a lot of dude ranches in the area."

Following her directions, Toby made a right turn onto the interstate and headed west for a short distance. As he did, he looked out over a wide stretch of flat land that ran all the way to the base of the mountains. He said, "My God, look at that."

A wind had kicked up at least a dozen dust devils that jumped and skittered over the arid landscape, miniature tornadoes that sprang into existence, darted along for a few hundred yards, and then fell apart. Toby remembered the dust devil that had blown past him up in the Panhandle, on the farm that had belonged to his mother. That one hadn't amounted to much, but these were more impressive, swirling yellow-brown columns that rose into the air and spun fiercely for a few moments, no less beautiful in their own stark way for the short time they whirled and danced before the vagrant breezes tore them apart forever.

Toby had never seen anything like them before.

"Your turn's coming up," Dana said.

"Oh, yeah." Toby sent the pickup down the exit ramp.

The two-lane highway meandered into the mountains, twisting and turning, following the valleys and canyons between the rugged peaks. Not much traffic. Toby saw only a few other cars and pickups and SUVs. Some of the foothills were topped by clusters of antenna towers, and they passed a large group of power-generating windmills, the huge vanes ceaselessly turning in the West Texas wind. Those signs of modern technology seemed out of place in this rugged landscape which otherwise looked much as it must have a hundred or a hundred and fifty years earlier, when the Comanche and the Apache rode it. Toby had never before seen a place where the land seemed so much more important than the transitory things built upon it. The whole idea made him a little uncomfortable.

After driving through the mountains for what seemed like hours, they neared Fort Davis. As they approached the town from the east, Toby spotted something odd on top of one of the mountains to the north: a large white dome, shining in the late afternoon sun.

"What's that?" he said, pointing.

"McDonald Observatory."

"Huh. Yeah, I've heard of it. I guess that's a good place for looking at the sky, on top of a mountain like that."

They passed the turn-off that led to the historic site where the old fort had been located, as well as the scenic loop through the mountains. Toby wasn't much for sightseeing, but under other circumstances, he wouldn't have minded taking a closer look at that observatory.

Right now, though, they had more important things to worry about, like hiding out from the three men who wanted to kill them and take their money.

It *was* their money now, his and Dana's. Gary and Walt had thrown in with Larry, and there would be no more talk of paying them off, not if he had anything to say about it. Of course, he probably didn't, since Dana was still running things, but he planned to make his opinion known.

"There are only a few motels here, and a couple of old hotels downtown by the courthouse," Dana said. "They'll all be booked up. We might find a spot in an RV park, though."

"That'll do. We can sleep in the back with the dogs and the money for company."

"I suppose."

"How long do we stay here?"

"I don't know," Dana said, and Toby didn't like the uncertainty he heard in her voice. He would rather she was firm and decisive. But after everything that had happened over the past few weeks, he could understand why she might be a little shaky. "They may have seen which way we went. They may not be more than a half-hour or so behind us. Or we may have given them the slip, and we could stay here for weeks without them showing up. There's just no way to know."

"We could keep moving. Spend the night here and then go on. What's south of here?"

"The Big Bend, and then Mexico. A lot of nothing."

"Mexico," Toby said. "That sounds romantic."

"Not what you can get to from here. It's not like Acapulco or Cancun. It's like this—" She waved a hand at their surroundings. "Only a lot worse. Drug runners and farmers who are slowly starving to death. No, Toby, we don't want to cross the river into Mexico."

He shrugged. "Okay. How about we work our way west toward El

Paso, sticking to the back roads? Or go back east toward San Antonio? They might have a harder time finding us in a place with a lot more people. We could blend in."

"Maybe ... We'll spend the night and see what happens."

They drove past Barry Scobee Mountain and the highway turned into Fort Davis's main street that led straight to the county courthouse. When they reached the square, Toby saw to his surprise that the roads on three sides of it were dirt. Talk about a place being in the boonies. Most of the parking places along the street were taken, but he found an empty one and maneuvered the pickup into it. When they got out, he found that the air was noticeably cooler.

"It's the elevation," Dana said when he mentioned that. "We're almost as high here as Denver. It's cool enough the dogs will be all right in the back for a while."

They went into the Old Texas Inn and Fort Davis Drugs, which had hotel rooms on the second floor and a drugstore and café on the first. The place was busy, and no one paid any attention to them. They ordered sandwiches and drinks at a long wooden drugstore counter and carried them to carved wood booths to eat. The place was touristy, all right, but it had an underlying air of solidity and permanence to it, as well.

Before they left, Dana asked the local girl working at one of the souvenir counters about RV parks in the area. She directed them back to the eastern edge of town. "Don't know if you'll find a place this late, though," she said.

The brief, high mountain dusk was on the land as they came out. It would be dark in no time. Toby had to turn on the headlights as he drove back to the edge of town.

Luck was with them. They found a park with a few openings left and pulled the pickup into one of the spaces. There were water and electric hook-ups, but they didn't need those, just a place to walk the dogs and then get some sleep. Toby took care of that chore and then fed them some of the dog food remaining from the supplies they'd bought in Pecos. He kept his eyes open the whole time and was very aware of the hard lump in his trousers pocket made by the revolver, but he didn't see any sign of Larry, Walt, and Gary.

When he got back to the pickup, Dana was already sound asleep, stretched out on a pallet she had made out of some blankets. Toby crawled up next to her, and Max and Clifford snuggled in next to him.

He'd be crawling with fleas by morning, but if that was the worst problem he had, he'd take it.

<h2 style="text-align:center">4.</h2>

He was right. He itched when he woke up. But he was cold, too, and the warmth of the dogs' bodies felt good.

The next thing he became aware of was that Dana was gone.

He rolled over and sat up, looking hurriedly around the back of the pickup. Light came in through the windows on the sides, but it was faint enough so that he knew the hour was still early. He scooted toward the door at the back. The dogs tried to follow him, but he pushed them back and said, "Not now, guys. Where'd your mama go?"

Toby swung the door open and started to slide out, but he stopped with his legs still dangling. About fifty yards away, right behind the RV park office, was a cinder-block building with a sign on it that read RE-STROOMS AND SHOWERS. Dana was coming out the door. She wore clean clothes and had a towel in her hand with which she rubbed at her damp hair. The sun had not yet climbed over the foothills to the east, so everything was gray and shadowy with dawn light. Toby saw nothing else moving except Dana. The park seemed to still be asleep.

Gary and Walt came around the corner of the cinder-block bathhouse and closed in on her before Toby could do anything except widen his eyes in surprise. He opened his mouth to yell a warning, but it was too late. He dropped to the ground and jerked the revolver from his pocket as Walt clamped a hand over Dana's mouth and Gary roughly pulled her arms behind her back and pinioned her wrists.

Movement from his left made Toby pivot in that direction. He saw Larry step out of some trees about fifteen feet away. Larry had a gun in his hand, and the weapon was leveled at Toby. But Toby's arm was up, too, extended straight out from his body with the revolver held firmly in his hand. He saw Larry's face, pale and ghostly in the gray dawn, over the barrel.

"Hold it, kid," Larry said. "Don't shoot."

"Why the hell not?" Toby said.

"Because no matter where you hit me, I'll live long enough to kill you, too, and then Gary and Walt will kill Dana and take the money."

"Yeah, but you won't have any of it. You'll be dead."

"Might be worth it to know I'd settled things with you and her."

"I don't think so," Toby said. "You're just like everybody else. You want the money most of all."

A grin stretched Larry's face. "Yeah, you're right about that. Where is it, anyway? In the pickup?"

Toby ignored the question and said, "How do we work this?"

"Yeah, you're smart," Larry said. "You figured already we want to make a trade. The money for Dana."

"And a promise that you'll leave us alone from now on."

"Sure. Once we've got the money, I don't care what you do. Neither do Gary and Walt."

"Let her go, then. Let her go now, and we'll give you the four hundred grand and drive away."

Larry shook his head. "It's not four hundred anymore, kid. The whole thing. All the money, or no deal."

Toby took a deep breath and said, "That's not fair. That leaves us with nothing."

"Nothing but each other, and your lives. Think that's worth it?"

Toby didn't have to think about it. "Let Dana go first."

"No. Get the money."

Toby hesitated, and Walt said suddenly, "Larry. Somebody's coming."

For a second Toby thought it might be a trick, but then he heard the car's engine and saw the flash of headlights as somebody turned in at the park's entrance. Larry lowered the gun and stepped back into the shadow of the trees. Toby took a chance and looked. The car pulling into the park had lights on top of it.

At this point, none of them wanted anything to do with the cops.

Toby stuck the revolver in his pocket and sat down on the lowered tailgate of the pickup. Dana, Gary, and Walt stepped into the bathhouse for a moment, and when they emerged, they were walking together like friends or family, with no sign of guns or coercion. The scene in the park, so tense a moment earlier, was peaceful again. The cop car came to a stop beside the office, and a uniformed officer got out and went into the building. There didn't seem to be anything urgent about his mission, whatever it was.

"That was smart, kid," Larry said as he came out of the trees, hands in his pockets, looking for all the world like he was just out for a morning stroll. He paused close to Toby and rocked back and forth on his heels, looking around as if in appreciation of all the early morning mountain splendor surrounding them. "We'll have to do this later, somewhere else."

"You won't hurt Dana?"

"No reason to, now that you've agreed to be smart and give us the money."

"It has to be somewhere out in the open, where you can't double-cross us."

"Now, Toby," Larry said with a grin. "Would we do that?"

Toby ignored that and said, "Up there."

"Where?"

Toby pointed. "On top of that mountain. The observatory."

Larry looked where he was pointing. After a couple of seconds he said, "Yeah, I guess that'll be all right. An hour from now? You bring the money and we'll bring Dana?"

"Deal," Toby said.

Thirteen

1.

He fought against panic as he watched Dana and the three men walk out of the RV park. Larry must have told Dana what was going on, because just before they left, she looked toward Toby and gave a tiny nod, an indication that she agreed with his decision. An indication, as well, that she trusted him.

She had no choice but to trust him. Her life was in his hands.

And it wasn't fair. He was barely twenty years old. He shouldn't be going up against hardened criminals twice his age. All he'd wanted to do when he left Oklahoma was find his mother. Well, find her and pay her back for abandoning him. He hadn't thought any farther than that. And just when he thought he was on the verge of accomplishing that goal, everything had changed and he'd been swept along into a bunch of shit that he couldn't control and didn't even fully understand. He wondered what would happen if he got behind the wheel of the pickup and just drove off and never came back.

Dana would die, for one thing. And Toby still wouldn't have any peace, because those three psychos would come after him anyway. They would never stop until they had the money … or until they were dead.

Toby didn't have any appetite, didn't worry about breakfast. He walked the dogs, impatient for them to finish, and then hustled them back into the pickup. He checked the revolver and got one of Dana's automatics and put it on the seat next to him along with the shotgun. He didn't trust Larry. Treachery was in the man's nature, and getting the money might not be enough. In Larry's twisted mind, he was the one sinned against, even though everything went back to his double-cross after the bank job in San Antonio. He might have to have revenge, too, before he was satisfied.

Toby stopped the pickup next to the office. The cop who had driven up earlier was gone. Toby went inside and took a brochure from the counter. It had a map showing the scenic loop through the Davis Mountains. McDonald Observatory was on a small road that formed a spur off the main loop.

The old man behind the counter said, "Goin' up to the observatory?"

"I was thinking about it," Toby said.

"They ain't open yet. Don't open 'til nine." It was a few minutes after seven o'clock.

"Well, maybe I'll get an early start," Toby said as he stuffed the brochure in his pocket. He started out, then paused. "Say, I thought I saw a police car here a little while ago. Wasn't any trouble, was there?"

The old man waved a liver-spotted hand. "Oh, no. Deppity just stops by here ever' mornin' to say howdy. Him and my boy Carl played football together back in high school. Six-man ball, you know. Ain't enough kids around here for the other kind. Carl's been gone ..." The old man looked up at the ceiling as he thought. "Nearly nine years now. Cancer got him. Yes, sir, the Big C."

"Uh-huh," Toby said. "Sorry."

"Anyway, his friends still look after me, you know. Well, you have a good trip up to Mount Locke."

"Thanks." Toby left before the old man could start in on something else.

He wasn't sure how long it would take to drive to the observatory, but he figured he could do it in less than an hour. After all, he could see the damned thing from the town, perched up there on the mountaintop. But the time passed more quickly than he had thought it would as he followed the winding road, and he didn't seem to be getting any closer to his destination. It still floated up there high above him, sometimes visible, sometimes not, depending on where the road ran.

He got even more worried and convinced himself that he had missed the turn for the spur road that would take him to the observatory. But then the turn-off appeared and he relaxed a little.

The grade became steeper, and the pickup's engine labored some as it climbed toward the top, winding around the slopes of Mount Locke. Toby leaned forward in the seat as if that would help the pickup make the ascent. His fists were tight around the steering wheel.

He checked his watch. Fifty-five minutes had passed since Larry had told him to be at the observatory in an hour. But they wouldn't hold him to that, not right to the minute. After all, he still had the money. That fact was enough to buy him some leeway. But with Dana's life riding on this rendezvous, he didn't want to be too late. No point in pushing fate.

He had done enough of that already in the past few weeks.

He was a little surprised when he came to a parking area with a large building nearby in some pine trees. The observatory was still well above him. According to a sign at the entrance to the parking lot, this was the visitor's center. As the old man at the RV park had said, the place didn't open until nine o'clock. All visitors had to park and check in here, and then walk the remaining distance to the observatory itself.

Only one vehicle was in the parking lot—the van that Toby had seen back in Pecos.

It was parked at the far end of the lot. Toby turned in and parked at the near end, putting several hundred feet of asphalt between them. He had thought there would be more people around, but there was nothing he could do about it now. He cut the engine and then took a deep breath. The air was cold, not at all like Texas in the summer. But that was normal for these high elevations, he supposed. He opened the door of the pickup and stepped out.

Keeping the body of the pickup between him and the van, just in case one of the others tried to pick him off, he went to the back and opened it. The suitcases containing the money were within easy reach. He pulled out one and then the other and placed them on the ground. Doors opened and shut at the other end of the parking lot.

He drew the revolver and faced them, squinting against the glare of the sun. It cast a beautiful early morning glow over the mountains, but Toby wished it were in a different place right now. He didn't need the added distraction.

Larry stood beside the van with Dana. Walt was at the front end of the vehicle, Gary at the back. Both of them were ready to duck behind it and use it for cover if they needed to. No guns were in sight, though, except the one in Toby's hand. He slipped it back into his pocket.

Dana seemed to be cold in the short-sleeved shirt she wore. She rubbed her arms for warmth. Toby thought she looked all right, like they hadn't hurt her.

"Okay, Toby," Larry called over the length of the parking lot. "Bring us the suitcases."

Toby shook his head. "No. Send Dana over here."

Larry laughed. "I don't think so. If we do that, you'll just grab those bags, throw them back in the pickup, and take off. Then the whole crazy business starts over."

Toby thought about it for a moment, then said, "Okay. Stay there."

He picked up one of the suitcases and started walking toward them.

He stopped when he was halfway there and set the bag on the asphalt.

"I'm going back to the pickup," he said. "You and Dana come get this bag. She stays in the middle while you take it back over there. Then I bring the second bag out and Dana comes back to the pickup with me. You can come get the second bag then."

Larry thought it over and then nodded. "Sounds like a plan to me. Let's get started before somebody else shows up."

Toby agreed with that. None of them needed any witnesses to this trade. He backed toward the pickup, and when he got there, Larry and Dana started forward.

He could see her better now as the sun rose higher, striking brilliant highlights in her blond hair. She was tired and scared and hurting, but there was something else on her face, too.

Anger. She was mad, mad as hell. And Toby didn't blame her.

The two of them came to a stop beside the suitcase. Larry started to bend down and reach for the handle, but Dana said, "Wait a minute. Can I ... can I hold it just for a minute before you take it back?"

Larry laughed and said, "Hell, no."

"It won't take long," Dana said. She reached down before he could stop her and grasped the handle of the suitcase ...

And brought it up fast as she twisted in a hard turn, slamming the bag across Larry's face as hard as she could.

2.

The suitcase burst open under the impact and bundles of cash flew everywhere. Larry stumbled backward and landed hard on the pavement. One of the other men—Toby never knew which one—yelled, "Hey!"

Dana dropped the open suitcase and sprinted for the trees near the visitors' center. Toby was glad he had practiced getting the gun out in a hurry. He drew it now as Larry started to get up and shot him in the chest, the report heartbreakingly sharp in the thin mountain air. Larry sat down hard.

Another gun went off and a bullet thudded into the body of the pickup. Toby twisted, saw flickers of movement as Gary and Walt tried to get behind the van. He fired without aiming, since there was no time for that. Gary stumbled and fell against the back of the van. He put a hand on it, trying to keep his balance, but he slipped and fell face-first to the pavement.

That left Walt, and for a second Toby was tempted to try to keep him pinned down behind the van while Dana made her way back to the pickup so that they could get out of here. But if they left Walt alive, he would come after them. Toby was as sure of that as he had ever been sure of anything. It was time to end this.

He started running toward the van.

Walt probably would have picked him off, but about that time Dana came out of the trees, having circled around. She yelled, "Walt!" and ran toward him, so that they were coming at him from two different directions. She was unarmed, though, so all she could do was serve as a distraction, and that was a dangerous job.

Walt's gun blasted twice, and Dana fell to the grassy lawn in front of the building, rolling over and over.

"Dana!" Toby shouted. He poured on the speed, rage and hate burning through him and giving him the boost he needed. He saw Walt through the glass of the windows in the vehicle and fired. Sparkling shards of glass flew everywhere. Toby couldn't see Walt anymore.

He skidded around the front of the van, his left arm thrown out to balance himself as he stopped. Walt was on his knees, blood pumping from a wound in the side of his neck. He stared up at Toby and tried to lift the automatic in his hand, and Toby shot him in the face. Walt went over backward and lay still.

Toby turned toward Dana, his breath catching in his throat, but to his amazement, she was climbing to her feet and seemed to be all right. "The others!" she said. "Check the others!"

Toby hurried past Walt's body, glancing down to see that his last bullet had struck Walt in the left eye and no doubt gone on through into his brain. The sharp stink of shit told Toby that Walt's bowels had emptied themselves. Walt was dead, all right.

So was Gary. Toby's shot had caught him in the back, just under the left shoulder blade. Probably right through the heart.

That left Larry.

Larry still lay on his back in the parking lot, surrounded by scattered bundles of cash. Toby and Dana converged on him, Toby covering him with the revolver. Even before they got there, Toby heard the harsh sound of Larry fighting to drag breath into his body.

They stood over him, one on each side. His eyes were closed. He was unconscious. The front of his shirt was soaked with blood. Dana said, "He told me they were going to kill us no matter what you did. Even if they got the money, they still wanted us dead. It was another double-cross. That was why I couldn't let you go through with it."

"You did the right thing."

She looked up at him. "It's always better to fight back, Toby. Remember that."

He nodded. "I will. But right now—"

"Right now I wish this son of a bitch was awake so he could see what was coming, but he's not."

"Yeah, that's kind of what I thought," Toby said. He had three bullets remaining in the revolver's cylinder. He fired all of them into Larry's head.

Then, since observatory employees were peeking nervously out of the visitors' center trying to see what was going on, they gathered up as much of the money as they could in a couple of minutes and threw it all into the back of the pickup. Toby saw the end of a bundle of twenties sticking out from under Larry's body where Larry had fallen on it, but he didn't try to retrieve it.

They got in the pickup. Toby started it, backed up, then drove out of the parking lot and headed down the mountain.

3.

They didn't go back toward Fort Davis, figuring that any law enforcement response to the shooting would come from there, but instead followed the scenic loop north into the mountains. Dana said there was another road that cut off from there that would eventually take them back to the interstate.

"Are you all right?" Toby asked her.

"I'm fine. Walt didn't hit me when he took those shots at me. I got down to make myself a smaller target. I just wanted to get his attention off of you for a minute."

"It worked."

"That was good shooting. Maybe you've got a future in this business, after all." She looked over at him. "I'm joking, Toby. I still don't want you having anything to do with things like this in the future."

"You're not my mom, remember? We'll see."

He drove on, pushing the speed as much as he could on the twisting roads, and after a while said, "How did Larry live through being shot back in Dallas?"

"Pure meanness?" Dana shook her head. "I don't really know. He came to enough to get out of there, and he must have known someone who would hide him out and take care of him."

"Chuck," Toby said.

Dana looked at him and frowned in thought. "You know, you may be right. He could have called Chuck on his cell phone and asked for help. Dead, Larry wasn't worth anything to Chuck, but as long as he was alive, there was a chance he might come up with the money he owed."

"By killing us."

"Yes. We were dead to Larry as soon as we crossed him, even though he was planning to do the same thing to us. That's just the way his mind worked."

"It won't ever work again," Toby said, thinking of the way Larry's head had looked after those three bullets went through it.

"No." Dana drew a deep breath. "It's over. They're all dead now. I didn't necessarily want it to work out this way, but now that it has ..."

"You're not going to lose any sleep over it, right?"

"Maybe a little ... but not much."

"So we've got over half a million dollars, a couple of dogs, and an open road in front of us. What now?"

Dana leaned back in the seat and closed her eyes. "You decide," she said. "I'm tired."

4.

Toby got back to the interstate in late morning and turned west toward El Paso. They stopped and ate lunch in a little town called Van Horn. Toby walked the dogs in a vacant lot next to the café. As he did so, an elderly woman with a Chihuahua on a leash joined him. Max and Clifford growled perfunctorily at the Chihuahua and then went back to what they were doing.

"Hello, young man," the old woman said to Toby. She wore a cloth hat with a narrow, limp brim, the sort that Toby thought of as a fishing hat, although he didn't know where anybody would go fishing in this stark, arid landscape that was all deserts and mountains.

"Ma'am," he said with a nod.

"That's a good-looking pair of dogs you have there."

"Thank you." Toby got the feeling he was supposed to compliment her dog now, so he said, "That's a fine little fella you've got, too."

"She's a girl."

"Oh. Sorry. I didn't look that close."

"That's the trouble with young people these days, just glance at something and go on. Never take the time to really look."

"Oh, I don't know about that." Toby didn't want to argue with the old woman, but he couldn't let a comment like that just go on by.

She changed tacks by saying, "Hear about what happened down at the observatory this morning?"

"Observatory?"

"Yes, McDonald Observatory, down by Fort Davis."

Toby shook his head. "Sorry."

"It was all over the radio. There was a big shooting there. Three people killed."

"Do they know who did it?"

The old woman shook her head and jerked the leash, pulling the Chihuahua away from a patch of cactus. "Some lunatic, I suppose. The place wasn't even open yet when it happened, thank God. If there had been a bunch of tourists around, it might have been one of those massacres like you hear about where somebody goes nuts."

"Yes, ma'am." He tugged on the leashes in his hands. "Well, come on, boys, let's go back to the truck." He nodded again to the old woman. "Nice talking to you."

"Keep your eyes open," she said. "Really look at things."

"Yes, ma'am, I'll do that."

When he got back to the pickup, Dana said, "I see you made a friend."

"She said what happened at the observatory is all over the news. But from the sound of it, the cops don't have any idea about us being involved."

"With any luck, it'll stay that way."

They drove west. Toby turned the radio on, hoping to catch a newscast, but in this isolated area the reception was spotty. He got more static than anything else.

The strain of everything they had gone through had gotten to Dana. She slept as Toby drove. After a while, Toby felt himself getting tired as well. He saw a sign for a rest area and roadside park coming up a few miles down the road and thought he might pull over.

When he got there, he was surprised to see that instead of the usual picnic tables with awnings over them, the little park was furnished with replicas of Indian teepees. They were made of concrete, painted white and decorated with bright orange designs, and were open on the sides and tall enough so that travelers could stop and eat on the shaded concrete tables underneath them. Toby grinned when he saw them and pulled off the highway onto the asphalt drive that led up to the distinctive shelters.

Dana roused from her half-sleep. "Where are we?"

"Roadside park. I'm a little sleepy, thought it might be a good idea to stop and walk around for a few minutes. I'm sure the guys would like to stretch their legs again, too."

"Okay," Dana said as Toby brought the pickup to a stop in front of one of the concrete teepees. "Roll your window down before you go, though. I think I'm just going to sit here and rest some more."

"That's fine. You deserve it."

Toby got out and went to the back to get the dogs. They were eager to romp, as always, and he was sure they would find plenty of intriguing smells. "Look at the teepees," Toby said as he clipped their leashes onto their halters. "You think Indians used to live here?"

Max and Clifford eagerly tugged him away from the pickup. He grinned through the windshield at Dana as he went past the front of the vehicle. Through the open windows, he heard snatches of music as she toyed with the radio, searching for a station that would come in strong enough to listen to.

Toby went all the way to the far end of the roadside park with the dogs and then started back, taking his time, letting them sniff and piss on anything they wanted to. Nobody else was stopped at the park right now, so they had it to themselves. The highway dipped through a narrow valley at this point, with mountains shouldering in fairly closely on both north and south. The roadside park was on a little rise that overlooked the lanes of the interstate itself. On the far side of the highway, a little creek twisted along over a rocky bed. Its banks were dotted with thick clumps of cactus. The whole place was picturesque as all hell, which was probably why the highway department had decided to put a roadside park there.

He felt better now and wasn't as sleepy. He thought he could make it on to El Paso without any trouble. "Come on, come on," he said to the dogs as they stopped to perform a closer inspection on a garbage can. "We've got places to go, things to do."

Reluctantly, Max and Clifford came with him. As they approached the pickup, Dana opened the door and stepped out. She closed the door behind her and leaned on it with her arms crossed.

"I thought you were going to rest," Toby said.

Dana's face was pale, and the skin seemed to be drawn unusually tight on it. "I heard something on the radio," she said. "A station finally came in good enough for me to hear a whole newscast."

"Something about what happened at the observatory?"

"At the observatory ... and before that."

Toby frowned. He wasn't sure what she was talking about. He had an idea, but discarded it as impossible. It had been so long, and he hadn't heard anything about it ...

"The police have decided that the shootings at the observatory may be linked to an armored truck robbery and some killings in Dallas," Dana said.

Toby shrugged. "So they put that together. They still don't know who we are, or anything about us."

"Don't be so sure. They're speculating that the stuff in Dallas is connected to a couple of murders in the Panhandle, and the disappearance of a woman there."

Toby felt something crawling up his spine. "Still doesn't mean anything. They don't know Dana Carson ever had anything to do with Grace Halligan."

"No, but they looked into Grace's background and traced her back to Oklahoma. They found out she had a son and gave him up. They found out the son is missing, too ..."

Toby's hand tightened on the dogs' leashes.

"And that the foster family he was living with were all murdered a few weeks ago. Somebody beat them to death with a hammer while they were sleeping. The man and woman, and the two children of their own." Dana took a deep, shaky breath. "It's all connected, and the connection is you, Toby."

"They weren't my family," he said. His voice sounded hollow to his ears. "Not my real family. They never adopted me."

"They let you stay after you turned eighteen. They didn't have to do that. They must have felt something for you."

He shook his head and squeezed his eyes shut, trying to force out the memories. "No, they hated me. Just like Grace. They were going to make me leave. They said I'd been there long enough and it was time I was out on my own." He opened his eyes and looked at her. "Don't you understand? I can't be on my own. I need a family."

"So you killed them and left," Dana said, her voice little more than a whisper. "You went to look for Grace, and you would have killed her, too."

Toby jerked his head back and forth. "No! I never would have done that."

"I saw you, Toby. I was there. You thought I was your mother, and you were going to kill me once you'd fucked me and then told me who you are. But Roy and Hans burst in, and all that got pushed aside."

He dropped the leashes and pointed both forefingers at her. "You're wrong. You don't know what you're talking about." His hands shook. "My God, I've risked my life for you, more than once!"

"I know." She sounded sad. "That's why I'm going to give you a chance. I'm not going to turn you in, Toby. But you can't go with me anymore. I could never trust you now." She leaned her head toward the interstate. "You can get a ride with a trucker or somebody else. I'll give you some of the money, so you can get along for a while, go somewhere and make a fresh start. What you do with your life from here on out is up to you, Toby."

"No! We're going to stay together—"

"I can't do that. I'm sorry." She paused, then said, "When that highway patrolman came to the farm, he was looking for Grace. I think he was going to warn her about you and about what had happened to your foster family. But it was too late. She was already gone."

Toby put his hands on his head, ignoring the dogs as they ran around his feet. "You can't do this to me!" he said. "You … you can't just leave me here!"

"I don't have any choice, Toby," Dana said.

He lunged at her, his hands reaching for her neck.

All this time she had kept her arms folded across her chest. Now she uncrossed them and the little automatic in her right hand barked sharply. Toby felt a heavy thud against his chest and went over backward, sitting down hard so that his head struck the concrete side of one of the brightly painted teepees. He got his hands on the ground and tried to push himself up, but he felt weak and hollow inside and couldn't do it.

Max and Clifford clambered around him, licking his face. Dana lowered the gun and said their names, calling them. The dogs hesitated, then went to her as pain spread through Toby, radiating from his chest, a fiery agony that was transitory, fading into an even more horrible numbness.

"I told you once I was dangerous," Dana said. "Don't say I never warned you."

Toby sat there leaning against the teepee and watched as she got the dogs into the back of the pickup. Then she went around the truck without looking at him again. He heard the door slam, heard the engine growl to life. In the fading light he saw the pickup pull out of the roadside park and onto the highway, picking up speed.

A gust of wind stirred past him, kicked up a spiral of dust, and then was gone.

About the author:

A professional author for nearly thirty years, James Reasoner has written many novels in a variety of genres. He is best known in the mystery field for his cult classic private eye novel TEXAS WIND, which was reprinted in 2005 by PointBlank Press. In recent years he has been concentrating on historical fiction, producing the ten-volume Civil War Battles series, published by Cumberland House, and three novels of World War II published by Forge Books. Currently he is co-authoring The Palmetto Trilogy, a trio of novels about South Carolina during the Civil War, with his wife, the acclaimed novelist Livia Washburn.

Printed in the United States
124878LV00002B/220/A